The Light
Beneath
The Light

First published in the UK by Beacon Books and Media Ltd
Earl Business Centre, Dowry Street, Oldham OL8 2PF, UK.
Copyright © Shereen Malherbe 2022

www.beaconbooks.net

Cataloging-in-Publication record for this book is available from the British
Library

ISBN 978-1-912356-50-8 Paperback
ISBN 978-1-912356-51-5 Ebook

Cover design by Sarah Nesti Willard

The Land Beneath The Light

A Palestinian reimagining
of Jane Eyre

Shereen Malherbe

To our land,
and it is the one far from the adjectives of nouns,
the map of absence

Mahmoud Darwish

Acknowledgements

بسم الله الرحمن الرحيم

Firstly, *alhamdulilah* for the ability and opportunity to write this novel. It is inspired and dedicated to the people of Palestine. To the women I know and am blessed to be surrounded by, your struggles, toil and strength that often goes unnoticed, this is for you and all others that are rarely seen.

A heartfelt thank you to Jamil Chishti, Beacon Books and team for being advocates and supporters. A huge thank you to Siema for her tireless work, passion and emotional investment in the project. The journey would be a struggle without your energy, dedication and support.

Thank you to my dad, Ramzieh, and our family who share their stories, hopes and homes. If it was not for the people of Palestine, it would cease to exist. May Allah reward you all.

To World Literature Today & Yousef Khanfar. If it wasn't for your recognition and understanding of my work on Palestine, I may not have been brave enough to write this. Yousef, thank you for your life's work, dedication and support for Palestine and its art.

Finally, this would not have been possible without the constant support of my husband. He has been by my side since our return to Palestine and ever since. Life would not be the same without you.

To my children, the future storytellers who I capture this for; for your history, present and future.

For Palestine and its people.

Chapter 1

KHADIJA REGRETTED NOT GOING into town with her mother. Boredom had set in quicker than she had imagined. She was tracing a family of ants across the floor as they scavenged for sustenance. Glancing around, she found the last crust of two-day-old bread, crumbling it and sharing it with them. She watched them carrying the crumbs, marching in lines through a small crack in the wall. Khadija wondered if they knew how tiny and inconspicuous they were in comparison to the universe. Khadija wondered if she was too.

Khadija was shaken from her thoughts by a tiny tremor reverberating through the rooftop floor. She froze on the old stone floor and pressed her hands into it. A deep rumble emanated from the ground. She stood up. She looked towards town and the streets in front of her house but her mother was nowhere to be seen. So, she turned around to check out the view behind her house. She glanced up to the hilltops, high above the fields behind her house. The fields behind the house began where the ruins ended. The ruins of an old stone building was not an uncommon sight in these Palestinian towns. Many homes had been demolished, either because they had fallen into disrepair or been cut off from borders that had swept around the towns. Her mother had said that the old stone building that was attached to their house had become uninhabitable and nature had taken over.

Had it snowed? Khadija saw past the mass of wild plants and fauna that had tangled and thrived over the ruins and saw something in the fields in the distance. She looked again. There was something near the hills. White balls of soft snow had collected in flurries and looked like they had been scattered in clumps across the field. She stared until her eyes were sore, trying to work out what it was she was looking at. It couldn't have been snow, she thought. There was never snow in spring. It was too warm. She had to get a closer look. Khadija had never seen over the hilltops before. It had always been a boundary she wasn't allowed to cross. She turned around to look towards the direction of town and she didn't see her mother coming. She knew if her mama found out she would be in big trouble.

Khadija ran her mother's errands through her head. She knew she would have enough time to get into the fields, discover what it was she was looking at and make it back home before she could find out. She ran across the rooftop and scrambled down onto the ruins. She slowly climbed along its perimeter wall until she reached the wall of the graveyard adjacent to the house. It was concealed by cypress trees so inside the grounds it was shady and dark. She crawled along the ground. Underneath, the soil was damp. The sunlight didn't penetrate through and she crawled along on her stomach to keep low and access the field. The light was blocked out. Her mind began to race as fast as her heart was pounding. The branches in the trees clawed at her hair and scratched her back as she went by. She didn't want to get further into the graveyard. She needed to crawl around the edge so she could enter the field and it was the only way without climbing down into the old house. The bumps in the soil made her imagination run wild. She could hear whispering; her name was being called through the wind whistling through the trees. *Khadija. Go home.* The cold, damp earth on her hands chilled her blood. *Never go into the cemetery,* the storyteller's voice repeated in her head, *the devils gather there.* At night she would hear a voice inside the ruins. The voice would tell stories that echoed into the night. She remembered the story of the devils in the graveyard. She closed her eyes as she crawled but that made it worse. Through her eyelids, she could feel their breath on her skin. She could feel them moving in the ground underneath her. She breathed harder and ignored the pulls and tugs from the trees until she fell into the field. She sat, out of breath outside the graveyard wall, relieved to have left it behind and be in the field. Khadija realised that there was a reason her mother sent her to bed at night, inside the house. She knew she shouldn't be listening to the stories the voice told from behind the wall. But there was something in her voice that, despite the danger, pulled Khadija outside where she lay as still as a stone, listening to stories spinning in the night-time air.

The long, unattended grass had grown wild. In front of her, she saw the fields and, in the distance, the unusual rolls of snow lay motionless amongst the grass. She picked herself up and dusted as much of the soil off her clothes as possible but the red mud had stained her clothes. She ventured out into the wide-open space of the field. Even the birds were silent. That was because there were no trees, so there were no birds, she said to herself as her little legs carried her closer and closer to the hilltop. As she walked, she looked back at the house and ruins. The house looked isolated from that view. It was separate from the rest of the town and next to the cemetery, which was one of the last places in the village. The roads were cut off by large boulders of concrete as they neared the hilltops and new barbed wire borders. Wrapped in a fog, the village was sometimes hidden completely in the clouds, as though it didn't exist when it was hidden in the mist. There used to be old Bedouin routes there but since the land was cut off, they now led to nowhere and Khadija didn't know of anyone who ventured past the blocks of concrete that had ever returned. The funerals always stopped at the graveyard and there the town finished.

As Khadija approached the blots on the landscape, her young mind began to unravel what it was she had seen from the rooftops. They were not rolls of snow. They were sheep. Dead sheep. Lying on their sides. Their bodies were stiff. Flies buzzed around their eyes. Khadija heard a sound from the hilltops. She realised how close she had gotten, how open it was in the fields. From her high vantage point, she looked towards town and saw a plume of smoke. What was on fire? She ran back down the fields. She climbed over the cemetery gate and ran across the graves, trying not to step on anyone underneath and eventually made it to the wall that she scrambled over until she fell on her roof. She stepped down the external staircase and ran out into the courtyard, the street. Where was her mama? She called out for her as the crowds gathered in town. Cars were speeding down there, the drivers jumping out. Broken glass was being crushed under her feet. She saw Amina and ran to her amidst the chaos. Market stalls were on fire. 'Mama!' she shouted through the people. She recognised most of the villagers, but they were busy fighting the aftermath of the fire and their faces were in shock. Wide-eyed, their mouths muttering under their breath, no one seemed to notice her pass through. In the distance, she saw a crowd of shadows walking away from the scene. She couldn't see faces, just the shapes of their backs and legs, disappearing over the hilltops from where they came.

'Khadija, are you ok? Are you hurt?' Amina, her mother's oldest friend, asked her, looking at her clothes and the dirt covering her face and hands.

'Yes, yes, I wasn't here. Where is mama?'

'She left me to go and pick something up from the sewing stall.'

Khadija thought of sky-blue thread. Amina grabbed Khadija's hand and wound through the villagers. Goods had spilt out into the streets amidst smashed glass, some were cleaning up wounds, and all the time Amina dragged her through so Khadija could only see and hear snippets of what had happened. They reached the sewing stall and her mother was slumped down with her shopping bags gripped between her hands.

'Mama!' She ran over.

'Khadija, are you ok? Are you hurt?'

'No, mama.'

'Are you bleeding?'

'No, mama, it is mud.'

Khadija's mind raced as she sat there. She thought of them the day before. On their knees, they had their *tatreez*. Her mother stitched directly onto *thowb*s but Khadija had begun with small pieces of scrap material whilst she practised.

'It is cross-stitch, Khadija. Begin with a simple cross and build up to this pattern. Look ahead to the fields. Can you see the cypress trees?'

Khadija nodded.

'That is what you are stitching. My mother taught me the same pattern.'

Khadija had poured the tea and stood over her mother, watching her effortlessly stitch the deep red thread against the black. She rubbed the stitches over her fingers and felt the texture underneath them.

'It isn't anything like mine,' Khadija complained. 'My pattern isn't straight.'

'It is just practice, *habibte*. You will be as good as me by the time we finish and maybe we can wear them together at the next wedding.'

Khadija laughed and took a break to drink tea. She preferred to stare out over the fields. She liked watching the colours in the sky change. She liked watching the clouds blow over the light blue skies and imagined how they were being blown by the angels. Her mother told her how the angels, as big as the mountains, guarded her against danger.

'Could we do another pattern? Maybe I could stitch the mountain and the sky.'

'Why not? Next time when I go into town, I will pick you up some blue thread.'

It was her fault her mother was there, collecting her blue thread. If she hadn't asked for it and been content to stitch the trees, this wouldn't have happened. The colour drained from Khadija's face. Her mother's shaking brought her back to the present.

'From where, Khadija, where is the mud from?'

'I saw something in the field, near the hills.'

'Khadija, I have told you never to go to the hills. Never cross over those fields and go to the hilltops. Even if our house is on fire, you run the other way. Do you understand me!'

'Yes, yes. Come, mama, we need to leave here.'

'Not until you swear to me, Khadija. Swear you will never go near there again?'

Khadija couldn't understand why amidst all the mayhem her mother looked more fearful about her trip to the field. She must have been in shock. Her face was sallow, her eyes focused only on Khadija as if there was another danger around them.

'Please, mama, can we go?'

Khadija saw her mother was trying to stand but couldn't move. She held her back and Khadija saw her wince in pain. Amina went behind her and carefully lifted her dress. Khadija saw a hint of her mother's skin, bruised and red across the whole width of her back. It made Khadija feel sick. Why had the sky not cracked open and angels come to help her? Amina tried to help her up and Sheikh Imran came to help with his son, Saladin, who was standing next to him. He was about the same age as Khadija. He didn't look as fearful as she felt, Khadija thought. She wondered how he looked so calm. A moment passed where he noticed her looking at him. He smiled briefly and then went on intently watching his father help.

Khadija looked up to see who had caused this. She saw the backs of a crowd of figures now disappearing over the hilltop, their shadows leaving town, the fire still smouldering in the background.

Khadija watched Amina's face. She turned to look at Khadija and forced a reassuring smile. Khadija carried her bags behind them as they carried her mother towards home.

'No hospital. I am fine. Go help these other people, Sheikh.'

'Well, let's get you home and out the way first.'

'No, please stop fussing, I am ok.'

'But what about the girl? She needs to be inside.'

'I saw something on the hilltops,' Khadija said, but no one heard except Saladin.

'What did you see?' he asked.

'I said, I saw something when I was on the hilltops,' Khadija repeated, hoping to get the adults' attention. It worked.

They all turned around and stopped to look at her. 'What do you mean, Khadija?'

'There was something there when I walked to the top. Something has killed the sheep.'

'Could it have been a wild animal?' Sheikh Imran asked.

'They were just still. Fallen.'

The grown-ups looked at each other and then whispered, but Khadija had heard. She heard a lot of the time she wasn't supposed to. Now they were away from the market, close to the hills. Their house seemed even further away from the village. Isolated almost. Too close to the dead sheep. Sheikh Imran would leave soon. There would be no one there with them. Khadija knew when the night fell on top of the hilltops, the lights would start to turn and they wouldn't cease until morning.

Chapter 2

INSIDE ONE OF THE oldest houses on the street, during the quiet morning that followed the eventful day before, Khadija and her mother were alone. They climbed into bed after praying the dawn prayer and spoke in whispers. She encouraged Khadija to read, as she often did. Khadija found reading effortless. She could read the Quran and she could also read the English subtitles on the TV. Khadija couldn't always remember what they spoke about in the hushed, soft time after their prayers but she knew her mother whispered protective Quran verses over her head, often having the effect of lulling her back to a deep, dreamless sleep. Khadija picked out the words she knew so well, their intonation and rhythm floating about in her mind. Sometimes her mother would speak to her in those moments, a cross between wakefulness and sleep.

'You were my gift from an angel, *habibte*, do you know that?'

Khadija used to smile with her eyes closed, imagining how much her mother must love her if she thought that. She was the age where she could walk and feed herself and help her mum, but she couldn't remember anything before that. She appeared one day. She wasn't like the usual children she knew of that are born and have a young babyhood they can remember snippets of. When Khadija appeared, she remembered being about five years old. She asked how she had come to get the scar on her forehead because she couldn't remember that either. It had been a childhood accident, her mother said. All Palestinian children had scars. So, for Khadija, there was nothing that began before it that she could ever recall. Of course, like any normal child, she asked her mama to tell her about the day she was born and how she was as a baby, but the few stories her mama told her didn't always make sense. She asked if she had a father but the way her mother spoke of that made her sure that he was dead because she never spoke of him as if he was absent, or away working like some fathers she knew of. He just did not exist and Khadija was just there. Khadija felt that she was possibly only half-human in the sense that she did exist; just not as complete and whole as everyone around her. She felt more like the shapeshifters in the stories she had heard about. The unseen amongst the living.

Khadija thought of the unseen. She was never alone, her mother often said. When they prayed, angels stood beside them. She often glanced behind her shoulder to see if the air moved differently, or afterwards, she scoured the clean bare floors for emeralds, rubies or diamonds that fell from their wings. But so far, she had found nothing. *Take me with you,* she would whisper. *Take me far from here.*

Khadija's thoughts were interrupted by the sudden onset of birds tweeting and rustling in the trees. She went outside and climbed to her favourite spot in the house; the flat roof that provided her with a vista of her street and the fields. She often spent time watching the birds. Crows and finches clustered in the trees. The hummingbirds were her favourite with their tiny bodies and beautiful bright colours, she often watched them drinking nectar from sweet flowers. She was always in awe of their beating wings, vibrating with speed in order to stay in one position. There was another bird she had seen but she wasn't sure if it was real or not. Sometimes she believed she caught sight of the bird in the tree outside her window. It never chirped or frolicked with the others, it just sat there amidst the highest branches, camouflaging itself in the leaves but through the dark green, Khadija could see that it wasn't like the rest. She often wondered where this bird had come from? It was like a bird of paradise, she had read. The martyrs were not dead. Their souls lived in the bellies of green birds in paradise. In Palestine, there were many green birds. She didn't know why the grown-ups kept saying that. She had only caught sight of its wing, or its body in the trees, but she was never quite sure it was that bird. The green birds she had seen in books belonged to far-away places she had never been to like the rainforests or the jungles. But still, she searched, sure that one day she would see the flock of green heavenly birds everyone spoke of so often. Had it flown in over the hilltops and never left?

Khadija knew when she was grown up, she would fly far, far away and see what the world looked like beyond her village. She would be like the birds. She would be free to go anywhere and then she could find her place in a world where people might one day know her name. She knew she didn't have the money to travel but if all the stories were true, there was nothing that would stop her from achieving her dreams. She was almost old enough for school. She had heard stories of those who studied hard enough, won scholarships, became doctors, travelled the world and saved lives. Her eyes lit up at the thought. Her mind had travelled with the birds, past the hilltops, over the mountains and to a place where she was somebody. Perhaps, that somebody would be Doctor Khadija.

When the sun brightened up the sky, Khadija washed and dressed for the day, willing it to be the same as it was before the sheep. Before the fire. But today was different. Her mother had used a chair to sit whilst she made her prayers. Khadija watched as her mother tried to dress but her movements weren't as fluid. Khadija noticed the slight creases in her skin that reflected the pain she thought she was always so good at hiding from her. Khadija did not speak about it. If she didn't mention it, it might go away.

'Mama, I need new sandals. These have a hole in.'

Her mother picked up her sandal and turned it upside down to inspect the hole.

'Yes, you do. But we will have to wait until I have rested and my back has healed.'

Khadija helped her back into bed. 'Don't look so disappointed, *habibte*. It won't be for long *in'shaa'Allah*.'

Khadija forced a smile, unsure of how she would spend her days alone. She and her mother were inseparable before so now Khadija had new-found, unexpected freedom which she used to venture further than she had before. She spent most of her days exploring. Since the ruins that the house backed onto and the fields behind them were off-limits, Khadija would go off by herself in the village. She wondered if Saladin, the Sheikh's son, would be out on the streets so she had someone to play with.

Khadija's village was unknown on most maps, except for the handwritten or the archived ones in the houses throughout Palestine. These maps exist on embroidered wall art in

Palestinian homes and in their hearts. They are spoken of between the elders and the families there, but month by month, names and places disappear from satellites. Soaring above sea level and hidden by its ranges of undulating hills, there were days when the mist rendered it invisible. What was normal for Khadija was that the fields were harvested sparingly. Since Khadija was born, the water diversions had made it almost impossible to harvest crops of any substantial size anymore. She heard stories of life before, life when the fields were full to the brim of produce that was sold far and wide. She sometimes saw young wheat pushing its way through the untilled soil as if no one had told it that the farmers were long gone. When farmers made a living off the rolling, golden fields of wheat and the villages were full of families. The natural landscape had always consisted of hardy fruit trees, olive trees and cypress trees that could withstand the land and its surroundings.

Khadija loved the outdoors. She loved traversing the fields and orchards and she was a natural expert in telling which fruits were ripe, which were almost spoilt. She handpicked sage and thyme that grew wild in the landscape. The wild sage, *marimia*, was used all over Palestine, stewed in tea during the winter months and used as an ailment for stomach ache. The small sweet pears that grew on the tough branches of the pear trees tasted of honey. The apricots and figs tasted like fresh, sweet jam. Almond trees grew alongside wild sage and thyme and when the wind blew, the air smelt of their fragrance. The symbol of the land, the olive trees, were most famous there, their roots drawing from the rich red soil that often stained her feet. Their tree barks attested to their hundred-year-old age and Khadija often felt them twisting and turning, wondering what they had lived through and if the stories she had overheard were ever as terrifying as they seemed. She picked the olives and filled up on them, unaware of what their trunks had seen. She skipped past the sumac trees, their deep red seeds a natural part of the landscape and food. Flavouring the dishes when the spices were ground down, they were also sold across the world and used for everything from flavouring to staining leather.

Ruins of a history long past existed in ancient crumbling towers that had always been part of the landscape. Khadija had heard of the graves in the rocky hillside, closed up and used as burial chambers but she knew the living did not play near the dead. The two worlds were never far apart. The very absence of life there reminded her of what had passed.

The roads had always been worn-out concrete, as scarred as their history and left for years without repair. Khadija, like most of the villagers, knew the parts to avoid and skip over so she wouldn't break an ankle running across the streets. The villas of the town were a blend of the old and new. There were flat-roof houses that were some of the first built there and the new villas with their pointed roofs and architecture dating back to the historical monuments Khadija had seen on the TV feed coming in from Jerusalem. They had arched windows and elaborate brickwork for those families who could afford it with their frontages, styled with lattice work and stone carvings. They would sit out in front of them in their stone court-yards eating together in the mild summer days. She wondered what it would be like to be part of a big family. Set in front or to the middle of the fields were the rural houses like the one Khadija lived in. There were the empty houses between them too. Families had lived there once but for every few houses that were occupied, there was a handful that had been left. It was once thriving she had heard, but now she seldom saw anyone pass by on the streets at her end of the village. The few families that remained lived in the newer part of town. No one really spoke about the ones that left. But their absence echoed through the town. Their absence was amplified by the overrun gardens and untended to orchards that Khadija frequented. She often felt as if she were in a realm by herself with only seasonal changes, sights and sounds of nature and the scent of fruits in the air. She felt like the place wasn't constant. It changed as the land heaved and sighed under its strain from the dead underneath it and the souls floating above it, but for Khadija, it was this rolling and crashing of the land that provided her with so much to explore. The harvest days were her favourite, because during the longer days she was allowed to stay out playing in the sunshine. The fruits became ripe and sweet and the fields turned into gold.

In the evenings, she would arrive home to the quiet house. Inside, her mother would leave out a plate of *medammes* beans or rice for dinner. She used to spend hours in front of the stove, turning simple local ingredients into the tastiest food Khadija had ever tasted. She missed those evenings. But from the fields, Khadija brought them their sustenance. This time, the young green wheat that had defiantly grown. She roasted the ears of it in the oven, the house filling with a smoky smell as it cooked. She pulled it out and added it to the chicken stock left over in the fridge. She cooked them together, making *freekah* soup, a staple food of these villages that had kept many families alive and fed. She shared it with her mother, followed by sliced honey pears topped with almonds and figs.

This particular night, Khadija couldn't sleep. She watched her mother wince as she moved. Khadija peered under the blanket and saw her back had become swollen and black. She didn't know what to do but she certainly couldn't sleep. She had to think of a way to help. If she was somebody important like a doctor, she could fix her. She crept out of bed and tiptoed to the rooftop, dragging her blanket with her to guard against the chill in the air. She settled herself down staring up towards the sky, thinking if she prayed hard enough then it surely must come true.

A star shot across the sky, making Khadija sit up and follow it until it disappeared into the blackness. Then, amongst the dead silence, Khadija heard a voice.

We all remember the Nakba, Khadija. The catastrophe. Do you remember your great-grandmother's story? It was an ordinary day on which the sun rose and did not foretell anything that would befall come the next sunrise. But during those hours, the shadows came down from the hilltops again. They came charging through Deir Yassin, slaughtering everyone in sight. Women, children, the blind and infirm. There were no barriers to their destruction. The girls were out playing in the fields when they heard the screams. Their mother dragged them into the barn and hid them under wet, red straw. She covered their ears and eyes and watched in horror as the massacre unfolded in front of her very eyes. When the silence ensued, she grabbed them and ran and ran under the cover of darkness until she reached another town. They had survived what many hadn't but your great-grandmother's survival had done too much damage. Her body failed her from the grief and shock and her girls became her carers. Sometimes their mother would wake up and forget what had happened. She would imagine she was

16

back in their family home, with her husband close by. Her brother still alive, her sisters and their children laughing and calling them in for food across the street in the houses they had lived in for years. But then she would remember. Their absence, the absence of the village was a void that has never and never will be filled. They live through you now, Khadija. Every Palestinian who survived the Nakba, lives with it in their veins. The pain is carried back to our hearts with each pump. With each morsel of food, or sip of water that the dead cannot take. Is there relief that we survived? Or are the promises of paradise even more tempting now we know our fate?

The story ended with the silence that had preceded it.

Chapter 3

THE LOCAL DOCTOR CAME with Sheikh Imran and tried to help as much as he could but he told her that she needed to get to a hospital. He suspected a small bone had broken in her back from the blow and she needed surgery to have it fixed.

'Can you tell that just from feeling?' Khadija asked the doctor, her mind briefly taken off the disappointment that Saladin had not come with his father.

'Yes, pretty much. Here, give me your fingers,' the doctor said, pressing her small fingers into her mother's back. But although Khadija couldn't feel anything unusual, she nodded enthusiastically. She watched as the doctor left. She noticed his well-fitting shoes and leather bag.

She walked him out and watched as he climbed into a car and drove off, back to his large house, Khadija expected.

Back inside, she asked her mother, 'When are we going to the hospital?'

'I don't have money for hospitals, Khadija, and even if I did, how would I get there? I can barely move around the house.'

'But I can help,' Khadija said quickly and willingly, without fully knowing how she could.

'You do help me, Khadija. Too much already for a girl of your age. Now, go and play. I am going to sit here and rest.'

'Shall I bring our sewing? I could sit with you?'

Now her mother couldn't continue sewing, there was nothing to sell at the market.

'I am feeling quite tired after the doctor gave me all these tablets, *habibte*. Do you mind if I rest?'

Khadija shook her head. She pulled out her sewing and sat next to her mother, but she couldn't get the stitches right. The shapes weren't forming. She wanted to ask her mama for help but she was sleeping soundly in her chair and she didn't want to disturb her. She slept until late, so Khadija missed dinner but managed to find some dried dates in the cupboard instead.

Khadija passed the days as best as she could. Amina dropped some bread and cooked meals off on her way back from the bakery. Khadija enjoyed those brief moments that Amina was there. She often told Khadija about what had happened in town and what was happening in everyone's lives and it made Khadija's world feel a bit bigger.

When Amina had put her mama down to sleep, Khadija took the opportunity to ask her, 'What will happen if she doesn't get to a hospital?'

'I don't know. I am trying to raise some money to get her there. Imran is too but she will need a pass to enter Jerusalem to visit the hospital.'

'If I were a doctor, I would come and help people who needed it. I wouldn't want them to pay me.'

'I know you wouldn't, dear, because you have a beautiful heart. And maybe one day, you will be a doctor and you will be able to help others.'

19

'Yes, I could,' Khadija said, 'I could study. I could read books. I can read.'

'Yes, that is the best way to start.'

'Where would I get books from?'

'Let me see what I can find for you.'

When Amina left, Khadija thought about becoming a doctor again. She thought about how she could then help her mum and others like her. She could be the one to save people. Then it wouldn't matter if the shadows came down from the hilltops because Khadija would be ready.

She waited for Amina to come back to the house. The next day, she woke up and made her and her mother breakfast. It was a bad day for her mama and she had to help her to eat the small piece of bread and the egg Khadija had made for her. The chickens in the village roamed so freely, Khadija knew where they laid their eggs and sometimes, she would be rewarded by finding fresh ones close to home without even having to go to the market to swap them. Khadija pulled the fruits, nuts and olives, often trading them in town for goods they did need. It wasn't as much as the dresses brought in, but it was enough for them to eat. Despite these luxuries, Khadija couldn't rest.

'What is it, mama?'

'Here, it hurts,' she said, pointing to her chest.

Khadija had felt her heart hurt before too. It was mostly after what had happened that day. Sometimes in the middle of the night, she shot up from her sleep and her heart would pound so much she could hear it in her ears. It had become uncontrollable.

Eventually, a knock on the door came and it was a welcome relief for Khadija. It was Amina with some freshly baked bread and falafel.

'Abu Saleh has his market stall open again, so we have falafel,' Amina said cheerily as she opened the door, waving the bag of delicious-smelling food in front of Khadija.

Khadija was plating up the food while Amina walked over to the dresses hanging from the curtain pole. 'These are beautiful, Salma. Are they ready to go?'

'Yes, they have been waiting for them but I wasn't sure how I would get them to Ramallah now… after–'

Amina broke in when her sentences began to break up. 'I can take them. If your hospital trip comes, we can do it together, can't we, Khadija? Whilst your mama is being fixed by the doctors?'

Khadija nodded her head from the kitchen, unable to answer because her mouth was full of falafel.

'*Masha'Allah*, you missed falafel.'

Khadija stopped chewing and suddenly felt shy so she went to fetch some water and remembered her manners, delivering a plate to the chair where her mother was sitting in the lounge. Amina perched on the old sofa next to her. She always sat on the edge; Khadija did as well because if they sat too far back, the sofa gaped and felt as if it wouldn't stand up to their weight. Salma hadn't used it since.

'Oh Khadija, before I forget, I found this old anatomy book at the bookstore. It looks a little outdated but I am sure it might make a good start. And look, Khadija,' Amina said, flicking through the pages, 'Lots of pictures!'

'Ah, thank you,' Khadija said, the excitement almost bursting out of her chest as she grabbed the book from her hands and began eagerly flicking through the pages. Khadija looked at pictures of the heart. It wasn't as she had read in the Quran. It looked like a machine, a vessel of pink with tubes coming out of it. It looked soft. It wasn't speckled with sin. This isn't what she had imagined at all. Still, she read and read. Her appetite for learning unhindered, despite no formal education.

Amina had a way of making her mother at ease. They were old friends and Khadija sensed her mother relaxed in Amina's company. Khadija knew that Amina had been married and had been a nurse for many years, but when her husband died, she took it on herself to be a caretaker for those around her. Khadija saw this in her so effortlessly. With her mother well taken care of, Khadija took the opportunity to go outside with her new book.

Khadija sat up, startled by the noise. She looked around and realised she was outside. She had fallen asleep on the rooftop again. It was cooler outside under the stars than her cramped bedroom and up there she couldn't hear the sound of her mother's coughing. When she heard it, her heart would beat faster and a dull throbbing pain would emanate from it and be carried around her veins. It was during those dark moments that Khadija wondered if she took her heart out, would she be able to feel any more pain?

On the rooftops, she could see far over town. She could make out the taller, two-storey houses with their newly built roofs and their solid iron gates. How would it feel to live in a house like that? she thought. It was more like a castle than a house. And further in the distance still, she saw where she imagined the horizon would be if the hills sunk. She lived on the outskirts, the broken-down part of the neighbourhood. Sometimes, especially on nights like this where the wind was still and the sky was a deep black, the only light was the moon breaking through. Its light cast a grey shadow on the village in the distance but it missed her house. It skimmed past her and left her in the shadows.

Did you hear of the women that survived? They carried their babies here with nothing but the clothes on their backs. We made them dresses out of our clothes and made them fit by stitching flour sacks underneath to fit them. We gave them everything we could but it was never enough to patch over the scars that were torn through them. Many of them ended up here afterwards. Some are spread about but they carry it on their backs. You can see it in how they walk. You can see it in the dullness of their eyes. After what they saw, who could think of life the same way again?

The sound she heard that evening was different. It wasn't the usual twittering, carefree songs of birds before dawn. She wasn't even sure what it was. It sounded like a garbled squeak and then she heard the rustling of feathers and something banging. Again and again, she heard high-pitched chirps followed by the sound of slamming. She sat up on the rooftop. Her ears straining to hear what was next. She realised the commotion must have been coming from the aviary across the street. When Khadija had first discovered the word aviary, she was shown pictures of beautiful dome-shaped wire cages that towered metres high. Or delicate ornate structures housing one or two beautiful birds. This is not what the aviary across the street was where her neighbour, Taha, kept birds.

23

His house was a dilapidated one-storey house that was surrounded by wire fences and a large aviary. He had canaries, budgies, finches and then some unusual parrots or tropical birds that his friends had come across or left at his house for safekeeping. Khadija couldn't listen to the sound anymore. She was used to it in the daytime but she had never heard anything during the night. She threw off her blanket and took the roof ladder down into the courtyard. The cypress trees stood still in the windless night. She opened the creaking gate and crossed the empty road to the house opposite. A few cats darted away from the wall as she approached. They would often sit there. Khadija saw them waiting, listening and wondered how they incensed themselves with the sound of fresh food yet they didn't have the strength in their weak bodies to make it over the walls. Instead, they skulked in the shadows, seeking out shade in the day, waiting for one to fly free and they would take their opportunity. Khadija was stronger than them. She climbed up the apricot tree and then threw her little body onto the top of the mid-height wall. She could hear now an irregular sound of feathers beating, then stopping. She fell down into the courtyard and stopped, looking around. The house in front of her was quiet. The lights were off. It looked as though there was no one inside, so she turned her attention to the outbuildings.

A heavy door was left unlocked, revealing a dark entryway into the makeshift aviary. As soon as she stepped inside, she was breathing in seed husks and the faint feathers that drifted through the air. She tried to get her bearings. Objects covered the floor, so she looked down, watching her step as she went. A small window allowed the moonlight to stream through just enough that she could see a small light socket on the wall. She knew the electrics through the old houses were temperamental at best. Tentatively, Khadija reached out. She flicked the switch and after a short buzzing sound, a light flickered above. She could see cages stacked on top of each other filling from the floor to halfway up the wall all around the edges.

They looked at her startled, some flitted from side to side. In a cage against the wall, she saw a bird hitting against the cage door. Its feathers were bright green, its chest a deep blood red. Black was underneath its wings and its long green tail trailed behind it. It was now barely moving. She ran over and unclipped the door. The bird tumbled into her small hand and fitted snugly in her palm. Khadija didn't know much about birds, but it couldn't be native to Palestine. Its eyes were almost closed and its chest rose and fell, then became motionless. It was dying in her hand. Its legs curled up like dry stalks, rigid and rough. Its head fell backwards, almost disjointing itself as she moved her fingers, desperately looking around for somewhere to lay it. 'No, no, no, you can't die,' Khadija said. 'You are too young, just a baby.'

She glanced around, trying to find somewhere to lay her. She cleared an area on the side as some things fell to the floor. She pushed down on its tiny ribcage. She had seen it being done before on actors on TV when someone's heart would stop. Just a few short pumps and it would restart, she thought. She felt the unusual shape of the bird's feeble body under her fingertips, just like the doctor taught her. The soft, loose young feathers that stuck out from its plumage. She knew it had died. There was nothing more she could do. A wave of emotion came over and left her feeling quite sick.

Then she remembered what a surgeon could do. Some of the images ran through her mind. She realised what she could become. If she could just see inside. If she could just see how it worked, it would help her. She knew that to be a doctor, that's how you learned. She knew people wouldn't believe that she was capable of it. She wasn't even sure herself, so this could help. She searched around and saw a small but sharp knife left near an open bag of seeds. Her fingers were trembling slightly as she brought it and hovered over the bird. She pushed it down into the bird's chest and sliced downwards, opening up her fragile, almost leather-like skin, which was tougher than she expected. Blood rolled out, staining its red chest darker. Then she pried it open just enough to reveal its heart. A tiny heart, no bigger than her thumb nail. It wasn't the same as cartoon hearts that are a vibrant pink in that shape of two perfect bumps rounding off to a point. It was dark red, oval, almost like a thimble. Khadija was so engrossed that she hadn't seen the light switch on in the main house. She hadn't heard the main house door open, or heard the footsteps coming into the aviary. She hadn't the experience to know what reaction to expect after intruding on her neighbour's property in the middle of the night.

The door creaked open loudly. Khadija dropped the knife and turned round to a figure in the doorway holding a large, blunt bat above his head.

'I'm sorry, I– I– heard something, I came to see if I could help.'

The figure dropped the bat on the floor and rushed forward, flinging her body out the way.

'What are you doing here in the middle of the night, killing my birds, you sick child.'

'No, no, it was already dead. I was just trying to help.'

'I knew you couldn't be trusted. Come with me,' he said, stomping over to Khadija who had now retreated further away into the shadows. She darted out, knocking over some cages on the way. She was in such a heightened state she couldn't recall if she had knocked them over or was unlatching them as she went, as birds began flying everywhere. It wasn't the free-flying she had seen the birds do in the trees; these birds were flitting everywhere, hitting walls and falling to the floor. Some escaped through the door.

'No, my birds!' Taha said, jumping out, trying to grab them as they darted towards the ceiling, the light, the glass-covered window. He was frantically trying to catch them with his large hands. Khadija could hear him as she clambered back over the wall.

Khadija ran up the rooftop ladder and lay down in the dark, panting. She could see Taha restoring the mess. She heard the clang of cages and the screech of birds. She covered her ears and closed her eyes but the sounds disturbed the recesses of her brain. They echoed through chambers long closed and brought back nightmares so vivid she almost thought they were true. She put her hand in her pocket and felt the soft carcass of the bird.

The sun split through the horizon, shining through her eyelids. She awoke with a view down to the bird courtyard and it seemed undisturbed. The cats curled up next to the wall. The courtyard appeared untouched. The birds sang to the impending sunrise. At first, she thought she might have dreamt it and it hadn't happened but then the reality of the bird and last night reappeared, giving her a sinking feeling in her stomach.

She didn't know what to do so she hid the bird in her bedside drawer before her mother saw it. Khadija rushed to the kitchen, scrubbed her hands in the hottest water she could bear and prepared breakfast, carrying the breakfast tray of sliced apricot and some dates and some slightly hardened bread that was left over from the day before.

'*Salam habibte*, never mind that now,' she said, pushing the breakfast tray away. 'Help me to wash before prayers. I don't have long before I miss it.'

Khadija glanced at the sky. It wasn't quite full sunrise yet so she fetched a bowl of warm water and helped her mother to wash her hands, face and sponged her feet so she was ready to perform her prayers. She slipped her shawl over her head and prayed standing up alongside her as her mother prayed on the edge of the bed. When they had finished, Khadija turned to her.

'What is it, *habibte,* you look worried?'

Khadija stuttered and then answered, 'We have run out of money for bread.'

Her mother didn't answer, so Khadija followed her mother's hands and cupped them to the sky, waiting for her mother to finish making *dua*. She wondered what she asked for. Did she ask for her health to be restored, or her walking to improve? Or perhaps she asked for more money so she could stop counting sheikals every morning?

Khadija returned to her empty hands. If she had time and wasn't so preoccupied with the events of last night, she might have asked for help. Maybe for some more food, the type she smelt her neighbours cooking on a Friday when the smell of chicken, rice and roasted nuts wafted in through their windows. Dinner hadn't been cooked in her house for weeks.

Chapter 4

MONTHS HAD PASSED. HER mother had barely recovered. Taha still hadn't been over, so she was hoping that her mother wouldn't find out. She had opened the drawer a few days after she had stuffed the bird inside but it had gone. Could she have fixed it without realising and then it had found its way out and flown away? Khadija thought of many possible endings but none of them alleviated the guilt she felt inside. Was the bird dying? Or had she killed it? She couldn't piece together the night's events without them changing every time she forced herself to remember. She felt as tiny on the earth as the ants she watched in orderly trains, treading back and forth, carrying the crumbs of their pursuit on their backs. She was like one of the ants that passed through, but got lost from the colony and had to find her own way in solitude. She didn't have any siblings to entertain her through those long days. Instead, she occupied her own world built on the small knowledge she knew of her world. And the odd glimpses she had from the outside, usually from the aerial television channels that would occasionally tell news stories and show scenes from Jerusalem. Her mother would tell her stories that she knew from the one book that she read. It was full of stories of the worlds that existed outside of her town.

'I have decided that today is a good day for us to visit the mosque. It is harvest season so everyone is gathering together.'

'I don't think I am up for it, Amina.'

'Have you taken your painkillers?'

Khadija saw her mama nod.

'Well, I have spoken to the doctor and he lent us this,' Amina said, going back outside and wheeling in a chair for her to use. 'It will be good to get you out, *habibte.*'

Salma sat down in it and Amina covered her legs with a blanket. Khadija ran to her bedroom to get changed and pulled out her favourite dress that her mother had bought some time ago and she hadn't had a chance to wear yet. They left the house and walked down towards the mosque. Inside, there were blankets laid out around the edges with different dishes on. Amina and her mother went off to greet everyone and Khadija saw a few children her age playing together in the middle so she went over to join them and was pleasantly surprised to see that of the two boys and a girl, one was Saladin along with his brother, Karim, who was taller than him with lighter hair. They were the Sheikh's sons. The girl's name was Aliya but she didn't know much about her except that she lived in one of the big villas further away from her house. The afternoon passed quickly. The harvest this year had been good, the food around the mosque was plentiful and Khadija spent an afternoon playing and running around with the local kids. 'Do you come to the mosque every prayer time?'

'Not every prayer time, but baba brings us a lot.'

'Maybe I could come too and we could play this game again?'

Saladin shrugged his shoulders. 'Ok by me.'

His brother, Karim, shot between them with a paper plane in his hand and crashed it into his brother's chest. 'Did you feel that, bro?'

Saladin pretended to fall back, clutching his chest.

***

Today was the day they were due to go to Ramallah. Khadija woke excitedly, knowing that this day could be the day that changed her life. She could have her mother back. She didn't even have an appetite for the breakfast that Amina was serving up. 'The mosque has managed to save enough money from the villagers to contribute to you seeing a doctor in Ramallah,' Amina said, as she placed her food down and began to eat. Khadija imagined that when she took her mother to the hospital, she might see the doctors walking up and down in their white coats with their stethoscopes around their necks. She would be like them when she grew up, she would tell them.

Khadija glanced at her mother. She hadn't eaten either. She looked pale in the morning light. Khadija gathered the dresses up and the carefully written addresses and family names on the pieces of paper she had double-checked last night. She didn't want to mess up the opportunity to bring them their much-needed income and her mother hadn't been able to work as fast or as well so these were the last pieces save a few projects she had started but not finished. It hadn't helped that one night, Khadija, meaning well, had stayed up after her mother had fallen asleep, saw the black fabric and pulled out her mother's embroidery kit. She had seen her mother so often, so easily, thread the needle, puncture the fabric, pull it back through and create the patterns she had sewn for a living. Khadija knew if

32

she could do it even at half the speed of her mother, then they might just have enough to scrape by. She re-threaded the needle in the deep red and began, and the first few went ok. But then she lost her way, the thread became slack and then knotted on itself. She had to cut the back of it to release the thread which made the other stitches come undone. The shapes weren't geometrical or aligned. And worse still, she had ruined a good dress.

'Khadija, what have you done?' her mother asked her in almost despair.

'I'm sorry, mama, I was trying to help.'

'I know you were, *habibte*. It doesn't matter. You have a kind, good heart, protect it. Even when I am not here.'

Khadija didn't like her mother talking like that. It made her imagine instantly that she was going to leave her. And without her, there would be no one left and she would truly be alone. She gripped onto her tightly and wished that she would never leave her.

'Khadija, are you coming?'

Amina's voice broke the memory but that awful feeling of dread stayed and replaced her earlier optimism.

They drove in Amina's car, down through the road that led out of the village. As they approached Ramallah, Amina exclaimed, 'This is what Palestinian refugees create, Khadija. Look at this city!'

Khadija looked around at the crowds in the city. The cars choked up around the roundabout with four lions in the centre of the main street's intersection. Women with prams crossed, sellers and vendors went out into the roads. People sat in coffee shops watching the world go by. Official government offices sat next to residences. Fabric posters hung from high rise windows and rooftops, advertising businesses and Palestine's freedom.

They arrived at a modern building; a place of sand-coloured rock, a name Khadija had read before in books found in Palestinian houses. It was the museum of Mahmoud Darwish, the famous Palestinian poet whose home town was razed to the ground by Israelis. His poetry was considered a national part of Palestine, as was he. Khadija read the poems on the walls. The stand where his desk was placed was simply staged with a piece of paper and a pen. Could the world be changed with the pen? Could it have helped his pain in some way? Khadija wondered. She kept repeating, '*To our land, and it is the one poor as a grouse's wings.*'

If she could only get into school and gain qualifications and get a good job, she could leave. She could be somebody. The thought removed her pain, her nightmares. Could she ever escape it because she was Palestinian? And she knew that people would resist and write and draw, but they also were imprisoned or missing or worse. She had never left its streets before. As far as she knew her mother hadn't either. Maybe that was her downfall, that she stayed. She was too weak to leave, to pack up her bags and free herself by fleeing to somewhere new where she could reinvent her life. After all, Darwish said, '*To our land, and it is the one tiny as a sesame seed.*'

'*And it is the one surrounded with torn hills.*'

Khadija's stomach flipped. Torn hills. The words ripped through her. She felt the colour drain from her face. '*...the ambush...*'

Amina rushed over to her. 'What is it, Khadija? Are you unwell?'

Khadija couldn't answer. She felt dizzy. Her head kept repeating the words, *torn hills, the ambush*. Until her eyes closed and she reopened them towards a clear blue sky. For many people are soothed by clear blue skies, but Palestine had plenty of blue skies yet it didn't stop the danger. On days of clear blue skies, the bulldozers still came. They didn't only work under the cover of darkness. There was a boldness to the ongoing work to destroy homes, to destroy lives and inch by inch, square foot by square foot, the land was seized and more and more were left to roam with their belongings on their backs. This happened on beautiful days when there wasn't a hint of grey in the clouds. Khadija spent a few seconds staring at the blue sky. She brought her eyes down to the green plants and palms growing in the peaceful gardens of the Darwish museum. It unsettled her so much, she wished it would rain.

Amina and Khadija returned to the village whilst her mother recovered in hospital. Amina brought them back some food and Khadija helped her to prepare it. She hadn't cooked much and usually only helped with preparing so Khadija washed the rice and chopped the spinach leaves into small pieces. She peeled the garlic and savoured the smell of the cloves frying in the oil on the stove. Amina showed her how to prepare the chicken. They boiled it with onions, cardamom and black pepper. Then they added the chopped spinach, fried garlic and coriander.

Khadija couldn't remember a time before that her favourite meal had tasted so good. Afterwards, with her stomach full, she walked outside to the courtyard and cried. She climbed to the rooftop so Amina wouldn't see her tears. When she had recovered and wiped them away, she focused on the starlight and the heavens and whispered her secrets for the angels to catch.

The sound of the neighbourhood dogs howling and screeching disturbed her serenity. She glanced over the village to check if she could see anything. The lights above the hilltops began swirling round and round, throwing lights onto the village. She could hear the distant rumble of tanks pulling through the streets. The barking became louder. Her heart thudded. She hid under the blanket, listening to her heart until that was the only thing she could hear. She peered outside of the blanket. The figures from the hilltop hadn't appeared. The fields were empty of sheep and silhouettes. Tonight, they must be coming. As a dead silence fell on the town, Khadija heard the voice begin to tell its story.

Once upon a Palestine, there was a girl who could talk to the Jinn. Now not many children could but this girl had a gift, or perhaps it was a curse because you couldn't always tell if the Jinn was a good being or not. But this little girl wasn't like everyone else. She had a will as strong as iron. She wasn't afraid of the dark. She didn't believe in monsters. She had seen much worse at the hands of other human beings. She used to hear it every day and seemed quite happy to have it in her shadow. Until one day, she challenged it to creep to the top of the hills and bring down its secrets. The girl waited and waited but the Jinn never came back.

Khadija waited for more of the story to be told but nothing followed. She looked around for somebody, but all she saw were empty streets. Streets, she had been told, that were once full until people were snatched and taken to places that lay outside the boundaries of the village. Khadija's mind raced. She

36

saw a plane fly above. An odd time for a plane to be soaring across the sky, but it reminded her that she could leave. Her escape could be of her own choosing. She didn't have to stay. The people that weren't taken left of their own accord and some had never come back.

Chapter 5

IN THE WEEKS BEFORE Ramadan approached, Khadija listened to the melody of her mother humming her favourite Quran verses, helped her in cleaning the house, scrubbing the already spotless tiled floors, and planning their simple menu for *suhour*. Her back still wasn't as good as before the attack, meaning that everything she did was harder work and more painful, to the point where Khadija often just stepped in and did it for her.

'I'm sorry. I want to, *habibte*, I really do.'

'There is no need to explain, mama.'

'I thought the hospital visit meant it would heal but *Allahu Alim*, I do not know. Maybe this is my punishment.'

'You haven't done anything wrong, mama.'

'Never mind that now. Your uncle is coming.'

Khadija stopped sweeping the floor. 'But you haven't seen him in years.'

'Yes, I don't know. Maybe it is the upcoming Holy Month that has changed his mind,' she answered, but Khadija could tell from how she arched her eyebrows, she certainly did not think that was the reason he was coming.

'He doesn't live too far away, why don't we ever see him?'

'He doesn't stay in his house often, Khadija. He travels a lot for work.'

She didn't know her uncle, but she knew that when her mother spoke about him, her voice sounded uneasy so Khadija couldn't imagine what he would be like in person. She hadn't much experience of family so it had never really bothered her until she grew a little bit older and began to see the large family gatherings around the courtyards and the swathes of people that ate, spoke and laughed together. Sometimes they were so loud, Khadija could hear them from her rooftop. She wondered what it would be like to be wanted in a crowd like that, to have people know who she was. It was a feeling that made her warm up a little to the idea of her uncle's visit. Maybe he wanted to make amends for his lifelong absence? Although Khadija didn't admit it to herself, she felt that if he did come it might be an opportunity for him to give her mama some money so she didn't have to scrape by for their food each day.

On the day of his arrival, her mother was anxious as Khadija expected. 'Why would he want to come here?' Salma said, looking around at the place, her eyes darting to the cracks in the walls and the window bereft of any dressing. She smoothed out and patted the old sofa but it did nothing for its comfort or its look.

'Doesn't he have one of the grand houses on the other side of town?'

Her mother stopped and glared at her. 'I've told, Khadija, money means nothing. It isn't going to help you on the Day of Judgement, only our deeds will, may Allah save our souls.'

Salma was interrupted by a knock at the door. 'How do I look?'

'Older.'

'Khadija, I do not have time for this!' But it worked, Khadija thought, as she saw her mother's serious face break into a smile.

Just before Salma opened the door, she turned to Khadija. 'Remember to stay quiet and out of the way. I don't want him starting one of his rants with you around, ok?'

Khadija rolled her eyes.

'*Habibte*, please.'

Khadija nodded respectfully and went to the kitchen to pretend to occupy herself.

'*Salam*, Jahid, welcome, welcome,' she heard her mother say.

Although her mother had said it hundreds of times to all visitors, the sound of her uncle Jahid receiving such a kind welcome made Khadija feel disgusted. From the kitchen, Khadija could hear the usual greetings of *salam* and welcomes. She couldn't hear the conversation, only the odd words, but most of it sounded boring to her anyway. Work, the weather, news of people. Khadija moved closer to the lounge door and stood by the crack, watching them. She heard her uncle talking about his work. He was working away again, he said. Khadija knocked the door with her knee. She darted around the corner so as not to be seen.

'Are you going to be so rude as to not come and say *salam*?' Khadija heard him bellow.

'*Salam alaikom*,' she said, peering around the door and remembering her manners, so she walked towards him to shake his hand at least. He shook his head and waved her away with his hand. He hadn't stood up; instead, he pulled the waistband on his trousers up and shifted his weight to the edge of the sofa.

'How are you then?' he said, not moving an inch except to use his forefinger and thumb to rub at his nose. 'Up to mischief I hear, around old Taha's place?'

Khadija's face reddened. She looked at her mother. She knew. Khadija could tell by her face.

'I don't know what you are talking about,' Khadija said, suddenly finding her fingers pulling at the loose stitching around her hem.

'Aha, a liar as well,' he said, puffing out a deep exhale through his nostrils. 'I see you are raising her well. As God-fearing as you.'

Khadija could tell her mother didn't know what to say, her face was crimson and her eyes were tearful. Khadija straightened up and folded her arms. 'Actually, I was trying to save the bird, if you must know. I am going to be a heart surgeon.'

He laughed so loudly he spat his cocktail juice all over his already stained jumper. 'Ambitious for a poor–'

'That's enough,' Salma said, standing up awkwardly. Khadija could tell she was trying to hide her pain.

'You are the one who has black spots on your heart now,' Khadija said, pointing to his chest.

'Excuse me?' he said, dumbfounded.

'What you said about work was not true. I could tell you were lying because you started to sweat and the corner of your mouth trembled as you spoke.'

'Why you little–' He went to go for her but Salma stepped forward.

'Is this really the life you wanted? To raise this?'

'I think it is time you leave.'

'I knew it was a mistake to come here, but after Sheikh Imran mentioned it, I thought it my duty. But if this is the welcome I get, I will leave you both to it.'

'Brother, please, we are about to begin the Holy Month of Ramadan. Come for *iftar* one night. Let us make amends.'

Khadija noticed his shoulders sink. He looked as though he was about to soften, then he turned to look at her. 'You are the reason for this,' he said and stormed out of the house.

He only looked back to throw a handful of notes on the side, but they missed and scattered to the floor.

'At least he left some money.'

'Khadija, how can you say that?' her mother said, clearly not requiring an answer.

'Well, we do need money and he should help. He is your brother.'

Khadija thought it was odd that a grown man would work himself up in such a way and storm off. She even let out a short laugh. She hadn't realised her mother was behind her in tears.

'Why do you care about what he thinks?' Khadija said.

'It isn't that I care what he thinks, but I thought things might be different. That he would understand.' She wiped her eyes and straightened up as much as her back would allow.

Khadija had learnt that silence was the only way for her mother to calm down. Khadija flatly refused to go back on what she thought and they were often polar opposites when it came to agreeing on things. Khadija didn't feel it was necessary to back down and she certainly didn't want to lie and for her heart to become hard. Her mother had told her that lying was one of the worst things you could do. And Khadija knew she did not like her uncle. And she did not care what he thought.

After a few minutes of sitting down and whispering to herself, her mother became more relaxed. Her breathing was more rhythmic and she had stopped sweating and simultaneously dabbing her brow with a tissue.

'Maryam, the mother of Eisa, did not need anyone except Allah. And neither do we.'

Khadija's stomach grumbled, but she did not say another word. That evening, Khadija crept to the roof when her mother was sleeping and waited until the storyteller began.

Once upon a Palestine, there was a young woman who was an olive farmer as had been her parents and their parents for generations before her. Every day when the sun woke up, so would she. The light would follow her down to her olive grove where she would pick the most beautiful tasting olives in the world. How happy she was to have her family home and their gardens filled every year with fruit.

The gardens had been tended to for centuries. Year upon year of tilling the soil, planting the seeds, and then nurturing the seedlings until they grew into the olive trees that began to bear fruit. Each year they were pruned back and the olives were harvested. The roots in the soil reached under the hardy earth and thrived in the Middle Eastern sunshine. There was nowhere on earth that produced the same.

'Drink from it and anoint yourselves, for the olive tree is a blessed tree.'

And blessed it was! Each decade that passed, the family would work the soil and water and feed the trees, and each decade the harvest grew in abundance. The gallons of olive oil were packaged, the olives preserved and sold all over the world, making the land-owners wealthy, and this continued for many, many years.

As the land around them changed, they built stone walls with each stone lifted one by one to make walls that secured their beloved tree. But the stones were not enough to protect the trees or their fruitful harvests.

Leaves started falling off the trees. The soil around the trees became hard and dry and smelt like something the olive grower had never smelt before. An acidic smell hung in the air and each morning as the sun grew weaker in the oncoming winter days, the trees began to die before the olive farmer's very eyes.

She scrambled about on her knees trying to scoop up the fruits but they tasted like an evil she had never tasted before and spat the remnants onto the soil. Her hands had sunk into it and when she pulled them out, her skin was falling off.

Each morning her afflictions grew worse, but that didn't stop her from waking and going to tend to her beloved trees. But one morning, she awoke to the heat of a searing sun. It was as though the hellfire itself had lit the earth. The flames licked higher and higher until they were almost upon the house. She ran outside and saw the olive groves aflame. The fire raged from their gardens to the horizon. And there, over the edge of the horizon, were the shadows disappearing over the hilltop, leaving behind their legacy of ash.

Chapter 6

THE NEWS OF THE moon sighting from Saudi Arabia confirmed Ramadan had begun. Salma, on hearing this, was
busy adding the last few tealights to the kitchen table. They
were metal shapes of a crescent moon and star and for every
Ramadan Khadija could remember, her mother would light
them for *suhour*. They gave the kitchen a warm glow whilst
they prepared their meal together. It was a boiled egg with
some dried fruits and a glass of water or milk. Khadija didn't
have to fast as she was only a child, but she wouldn't have
missed waking up in the early hours of the morning to eat with
her mother at this exciting time. The dinner parties had died
down and it was as though they were the only ones awake. It
was usually just after the lights from the hilltop had stopped
spinning. The birds hadn't risen yet, the night was still black
and it felt hopeful and new. When a single bird began to tweet
and the horizon outside the small window began to lighten,
the *muezzin* would follow by calling the prayer. Before her
mother's back was hurt, they would go out together and join
the other villagers, praying together in unison. Khadija never
forgot the feeling of going out into the fresh air in the still dark
morning and being welcomed by the lights of the mosque and
the people inside it. This year, Khadija had a feeling it would be

different and she did not mention it to her mother, because she knew if anyone missed praying in congregation, no one could have missed it more than her mother. So instead, they slipped on their prayer shawls and prayed the dawn prayer at home, almost in sync with the mosque as they could hear the Imam say, *Allahu Akbar* which echoed out into the streets and sounded as if it would reach the tops of the mountains.

After prayer her mother would read the first chapter of the Quran; a Ramadan tradition of hers was to try and read the entire Quran, finishing before Eid. As she read, Khadija would fall asleep next to her until the heat of the sun warmed up the small room, signalling the start of their day.

They spent the days together once again and Khadija was relieved that her mother was in better spirits than before. Her happiness began to flow again once the devils were chained up and her mother's favourite month was upon them.

Jahid's money had stretched to buy some food for *iftar* for the first few weeks and that had alleviated some pressure off Khadija's mind and she knew that it must have done for her mother as well, allowing their days to be relaxed. Together, they would read Quran and make *dua* side by side on the floor. Her mother told her stories of hope and faith. They would watch the live coverage from Mecca and Medina stream into the room and fill up with the worshippers, as if they too were standing at the Grand Mosque in Mecca.

But the slow, contemplative days and hearing the stories of the Quran and its telling of the world and the wider universe around them had the effect of making Khadija miss roaming around outside. She missed the feel of the earth beneath the soles of her feet. She missed the delicate touch of the breeze on her cheeks. She could spend hours lying in the soft grass upon the earth, watching the clouds pass above her head as the sun painted its own ever-changing colours into the sky. Inside, she felt almost trapped between the walls and the house seemed to shrink around her. Sometimes she even imagined she could smell the fruits ripening on the trees as if they were close by.

During the evenings, she still went out to the rooftops hoping to hear the voice tell more stories that she could imagine and escape to, or wonder about. But each evening, the voice never spoke. Instead, she imagined Jerusalem. Jerusalem was alive at night. It was a busy city filled with tourists, locals and worshippers from all over the world. It was a place that, despite being so close, Khadija had never been to. Sometimes from the rooftops, Khadija thought that even though it was practically impossible, she could see the glint of the Dome of the Rock and wondered if one day she would get to go and visit it for real, in person. Her mother told her she dreamt of taking her to the place where their beloved Prophet Mohammed (peace be upon him) went on his night journey, only to ascend to the tops of paradise that lay far above the stars and how he met the other Prophets that came before him. Khadija could almost imagine what the winged creature looked like that carried him from the streets of Mecca to their homeland that houses Al-Aqsa Mosque. It made the stories come alive and Khadija felt her heart expand with new-found hope. It was no coincidence, she thought, that in that time she had read about the youngest doctor in the world being a Palestinian refugee. Her path was set. She was going to become someone and save her mother and maybe others and then everyone would know her name.

The evenings passed with the streets alive with people before dusk. They delivered food to one another and never forgot about Khadija and Salma. During the late afternoons, the gates were thrown open and everyone would be out delivering food. Khadija had helped her mother make some soup and exchanged it at the doors as meals passed over. The smell of the cooking was glorious to Khadija. She could smell it wafting down the streets and each night there were different dishes from different neighbours. Just as the sun fell down behind the hilltops and before the call to prayer signalled the end of the day, everyone was back in their houses. They ensured everyone in the neighbourhood had food before whispering their prayers up to the heavens and breaking their fasts.

The nights passed too quickly for Khadija. But the last ten nights brought with it its own wonder.

'Khadija, tonight could be *Laylat Al-Qadr*. Your favourite time in Ramadan. Do you remember?'

Khadija did remember that ever since she was young, they used to try and spot the Night of Power where Allah sends thousands of angels down to earth on this one night, where there are more angels than there are stars in the galaxy. It was one of her most favourite parts of Ramadan to imagine that the earth was so full.

'Is it time?'

'Let's go and see,' her mother said, and they opened the door out onto the courtyard. They looked out over the fields in front of the house where they rolled down towards the horizon. The sun was beginning to rise.

'Look, mama, no rays. The angels are blocking the rays!'

'It does look like a rayless sunrise, Khadija. This evening could be it. We don't have long until sunrise. Have you asked Allah what you wish for?'

Khadija screwed her eyes shut tightly and held her cupped hands out to the sky.

She returned her vision to her mother who was doing the same. 'It feels peaceful and calm doesn't it, mama?'

'Yes, *habibte*, it does.'

Khadija looked hard around the fields as far as she could see into the distance towards the horizon, trying to imagine the angels filling up the spaces between them as she couldn't see or hear a thing. That morning, the last sign that it had passed, happened; the sun rose like a disc. To cement Khadija's assurance that they had lived to see the Night of Power that year, the morning began with a gentle mist of rain that kissed her cheeks and the soil. This was the year her dreams would come true.

Chapter 7

KHADIJA WAS DUE TO start school. She was sure she should have started already but she knew it cost money and she knew that her mother didn't have it so she never mentioned its absence in her life. But now it was real. She guessed someone had paid for it, as her mama had mentioned that happened sometimes for families who needed some help. Now for Khadija, it was really happening, and she wanted to be ready to begin the first days of her education. After all, her education was the ticket to her dreams. It began with as much research as she could fit in. She started off small. She counted the beats in her heart when she was at rest. She counted the increase in them when she heard the tanks rolling through the village. She felt the vigour in her veins and the pulse throbbing in her neck when the soldiers raided the house down the street in the dead of night as she watched from the rooftops. She saw the breath change in the air of those arrested. It would quicken and dampen in the fog. She saw them kicked and beaten and watched how the breaths became sharp, their muscles filling with blood as their hearts worked faster under the adrenaline. Her eyes watched as the scene unfolded, the men taken. The women left behind in the house crying out into the night. Khadija placed her hand on her own timid heart quickening behind her chest. She breathed slowly, deeply, her heart calmed down and Khadija was resolved; she knew if she could control the heart, she could find her strength in the world.

She scrubbed her shoes until all the second-hand marks had been removed, but because the material was so soft, a few holes appeared in the toes. She took her mother's sewing kit and she stitched them up as tightly as she could.

She looked in the coin jar and there was nothing but a few sheikal and she would need that for food, so she couldn't use it to buy a notebook and pencil. She remembered the apricot trees near Taha's house. She knew they would be ripe. She went out and pulled them off, filling her basket before walking briskly into town. She passed the stone-making factories and saw the hillsides tumbling down to the horizon, marked by the skeletons of the trees against the pale sky. Her pace was slightly off she realised, and looked down to her oversized shoes. She stumbled on loose stones and lost half of the apricots down the steep embankment. She picked up the remaining ones and turned up at Hakim's stationery store. Hakim sat behind a table where the till was perched, reading his Arabic newspaper. From the date, it was already a few days old. His heavy, black eyebrows creased in anger as he read the articles. He slammed it down on the counter, which made Khadija jump.

'*Salam,* Khadija. What is it you would like?' His face softened slightly which gave her the confidence to go forward.

'I need a notebook and a pencil. I have brought you these apricots. There were more but I tripped on the way and they rolled down the hill,' Khadija said, tipping them out on the table near the till, only to watch them fall off under the counter, 'So I only have a few left, I thought that maybe it would do,'

Khadija said, from half underneath the table as she clumsily tried to put them all back on, rubbing off the dust and shavings that they had rolled in on the floor.

Hakim looked at the apricots and then looked up at Khadija. The silence made her uncomfortable. She had nothing else to give. She could feel her cheeks reddening. There it was again, her heart giving away her embarrassment. She turned to leave the store, darting outside to save any dignity she had left, when she heard Hakim's chair move.

'Come with me,' he said. She turned around and followed him, winding through the shelves to the back of the store where the notebooks were piled up.

***

School arrived and Khadija, despite being ushered back to sleep by her mother, could not fall asleep again after the dawn prayer, so she snuck out of bed and began to get ready. She had already been up for hours but her mind was racing. She had to be organised and make their lunch. She couldn't be late and she wasn't exactly sure how long it would take to walk there, even though that wasn't entirely true, she told herself immediately after having the thought. She had often wandered towards the school just to listen to the sound of the children playing in the playground, wondering what it would be like to go. It used to upset her so she had stopped that a while ago. But today, she was going to be one of those children in the school. Learning about the world through books and teachers. She had been up so early that she had made her mother a lunch just like the one she had packed herself and left it on the side. 'Mama, you have an egg, salad and fool on the side. Is that enough for you?'

'Khadija, you should have woken me, I was going to prepare your lunch today as a treat.'

'I know, mama, but I couldn't sleep. I was too excited, so I did it for you,' Khadija said, wrapping it up in plastic wrap so the ants wouldn't get to it. She instantly felt guilty for not sharing with them in case they were hungry and came looking, so she left them a few crumbs pushed back near the tiles. 'Plus, you would have had to get up so early and there was no need.'

'To see you off to school! I wouldn't have missed it for the world,' she said, 'May Allah bless this day and this journey for you, *habibte*.'

'Thank you, mama. Love you.'

'Love you too.'

Khadija skipped out of the door with a light heart and heavy school bag full of books and anticipation. Her heart was light. The beginning of her future was about to begin.

Khadija arrived at school with a pile of notebooks, a shiny green pencil case full of pencils and pens that she had successfully swapped for her apricots at Hakim's store. She went to wait in the playground and sat down, opening her notebook when a sharp shove knocked it clean out of her hands and into a puddle of stagnant water left from the rainfall the night before. 'What are you doing?' said Khadija, kneeling by the puddle and pulling out her now sodden book, without looking up.

A kick of her wrist forced her to land back on the ground, her face now dripping in water, her ears stinging from a sudden eruption of laughter.

'Murderer,' the voice whispered.

'I didn't kill it. It was already dying.'

'Maybe she was hungry,' a voice laughed. 'We had to pay for you to even come here.'

'Leave her alone.'

Khadija only heard the voices but she recognised this one. She knew it belonged to Saladin and instantly she felt better.

'Poor little orphan,' the girl muttered under her breath. She knew this one must have been Aliya. Aliya was always the one thinking she was better than everyone else. She was the one who lived in the biggest house there and her family owned half the fields behind it. She had helpers at her house and whatever she wanted.

'Aliya, leave it,' Saladin said again.

'Ok, goody-two-shoes,' Aliya retorted but she did leave. Khadija heard the bell ring. She looked up and saw Saladin standing there. 'I didn't need you to do that. I was fine.'

Saladin shrugged his shoulders and went inside the school.

Khadija's heart stung as she saw all the line markings had faded and were now barely legible. It's worth it, she thought. What would they all think of her when she made something of herself? Everyone would know her.

She arrived at class late and slightly damp. She noticed the teacher, Miss Ayesha, looking up at her. She flashed her a quick smile and beckoned with her hand for Khadija to choose a seat. Khadija smiled back, feeling relieved that her teacher seemed kind. Aliya turned in her chair and scowled at Khadija, even though Khadija would never have chosen a chair next to mean Aliya anyway.

Khadija sat on a solo table facing the front of the class. She sat next to a small window that looked out onto the concrete playground. Chalk marks decorated the walls and just beyond the high concrete walls, the trees grew even taller. She took a deep breath and settled into her chair to pay attention to Miss Ayesha and the words she wrote on the blackboard. She frantically scribbled and copied them down on some spare pieces of paper, taking only a few days to settle into the school routine and become used to the view out of the window.

The days turned into weeks but nothing seemed to sink in. Khadija found it harder than she thought to keep up. She would be sat there listening and then she would fade out of the classroom with its posters, desks and children. Her mind would drift back to the four walls of her house wondering if her mother was ok. Had she managed to make some food? Was she feeling lonely without her? The information didn't seem to sink into her brain and made her head hurt. The words seemed to float around the room and then drop around her without making any sense.

She hadn't learnt any of this. Everyone else seemed to be in a rhythm, they seemed to pick up where she had never begun and it didn't feel how she expected it to. She already felt behind, out of place. Stupid.

After class had finished, Khadija sat behind trying to catch up and rewrite her notes. When the students had left, Miss Ayesha came and sat by her desk.

'Khadija, is everything ok?'

'Yes, Miss. It's just I can't fall behind. I wanted to start ahead. I need the best grades because I can't get into school without a scholarship. You know my mother can't afford that.'

'Ok, Khadija, calm down, dear,' said Miss Ayesha, 'You have your sights set high?'

'I don't know what else to do.'

Khadija hadn't even noticed the bubble rising and exploding in her chest, producing a cascade of tears that fell freely now that everyone had left and it was only kind Miss Ayesha sat there with her, rubbing her forearm. 'Shush, come on, don't cry. Let me see what you are working on there and I will help you, ok?'

They sat together and Miss Ayesha explained where she had gone wrong with her calculations. They were interrupted by the sound of the *muezzin* calling out for prayer. 'It can't be *magrib* already?' Khadija said, looking up at the front of the classroom to the wall clock. 'I need to get back, mama must be wondering where I am.'

'I didn't realise we had spent so much time together. Let me walk you home.'

'No, it's fine, Miss Ayesha. I am at the end of the village and I can run quite fast.'

Miss Ayesha let out a short laugh, but Khadija was not joking.

'Thank you so much, Miss, I don't know what I would have done without you. My mama can't, well, maybe she used to be able to help, but now–'

'Never mind, Khadija, you don't need to explain. I will see you tomorrow, dear.'

As Miss Ayesha gathered her things to leave, Khadija bolted out of the classroom. Saladin's voice had stopped and the streets were beginning to darken with the onset of dusk. As Khadija approached the end of the street, the lights from the houses faded, the fields were now almost navy in the moonlight and she felt immediately nervous by the fact that no lights were shining from inside the house. Her step quickened and she barged through the door, tossing her bag to one side. 'Mama?' Her voice was higher pitched than usual, shaking with nervous anticipation of an answer but none came. 'Mama?' she called again, louder this time. A response came in the form of a moan towards the kitchen. She ran in and found her on the floor. Her wheelchair had tipped as she had reached for something on the side. Khadija felt guilt stir inside her as she realised it was the plate of food she must have reached for before she fell. She was too late to prepare her dinner for her.

She ran over and tried to help her back up. She noticed her skin was cold from the stone floor. How long had she been lying there? It was no use; even with all of Khadija's strength, she barely moved her.

'Wait, mama. I need to go and get help.'

Khadija's mind raced. Taha was closest but she couldn't ask him. Not after what had happened. She remembered Saladin's voice. Sheikh Imran came into her head; he would have led the prayers. Maybe he was still at the mosque? She ran down to the mosque but it was quiet. Dark. The main doors had been locked.

'Sheikh Imran, Sheikh Imran. Help. I need help,' Khadija said, banging on the door.

She heard footsteps inside, hurrying quickly across the carpeted floor. The door was unbolted. Khadija did not find Sheikh Imran behind the door.

'Where is your baba? I need help.'

'He isn't here, Khadija. I can help. What has happened? Are you hurt? Are they here?'

'No, no, it isn't them.' Khadija had no other option but to tell him, to let him know of her recklessness that had led to this. 'Mama has fallen.'

Saladin was already locking the mosque doors behind him. Khadija noticed that her hands were shaking as she tried to help him. 'It's all my fault,' she said, but he didn't hear. He was already ahead of her, running towards her house. When he crossed the doorway, Khadija had caught up. He ran straight over to Salma and held her hand. He spoke to her in hushed words and then lifted her under the arms. Khadija darted behind her and pushed the chair under her legs as he gently placed her in. Saladin was stronger than he looked. His mannerisms were quiet, understated, but she suddenly saw him differently. He tucked his hair behind his ears and instantly retreated when Salma was back in her chair. Khadija adjusted her mother's headscarf and unrumpled her clothes to restore her dignity. 'We should call the doctor, to check her over. She might be hurt,' Saladin said.

'Yes, yes, let me get the phone,' Khadija answered. She went to get the phone but felt her mother's arm on hers.

'Don't bother the doctor, Khadija. He is a busy man and I am fine.'

Khadija went back and forth pleading with her to just call and check herself over. She was sure he wouldn't charge, she consoled.

'Shall I call my father?' Saladin interjected.

'No, *habibe*, you have done plenty, thank you.'

Khadija carried on protesting with her mother until she noticed she looked tired. She should have learnt by now that her mother's words were always final. Then she realised it was just the two of them in the room. Her mother had thanked him, but she hadn't and now he wasn't there. She would have gone after him into the street if she could, but she couldn't leave her mother despite everything inside of her making her want to run out into the street. She imagined he would be past the gate by now. She wanted to throw her arms around him, to thank him from the depths of her heart for making the night a bit easier on her now tortured soul. She imagined him further away. Now, on the street. She wanted to thank him for the playground, for standing up for her when Aliya was mean to her. She stood there, imagining his footsteps fade as he walked away from her, noticing an absence she had never felt before burn into her heart.

She went to the door and peered outside into the darkness onto an empty courtyard. The lights on the hilltop switched on at that exact moment. She took her eyes from the courtyard and the street view and glanced behind her house where the lights started to rotate on the hilltop.

'Shut the door, Khadija,' her mother called weakly. She glanced up to see if there was any movement but it was only the sound of the turning lights. A constant whirring sound that she didn't know was real and came from the lights, or a sound her subconscious made up every time she saw them. She slammed the door and slid the heavy bolts across it. She retreated inside, made some hot tea and gave it to Salma, but she couldn't hold it because her hands were too unsteady. 'It's ok, I will hold it for you,' Khadija said, offering small sips up to her pale lips. She wondered if her mother was getting weaker; she had never fallen before. Usually, she could get in and out of her chair without assistance. 'Mama, do you need to see a doctor? Does it hurt anywhere?'

'Come now, Khadija, you know we can't afford to see another doctor.'

Khadija's stomach dropped. Her mother must have seen it in her face because she quickly followed it up, 'Plus I don't need to see a doctor, *habibte*. Just help me into bed and pass me the extra blanket.' Khadija put a second, thick blanket on that they hadn't had to use all season. But she could feel the cold from the floor had penetrated her skin and she knew she would need some time to warm up. Khadija switched the TV on. It automatically turned on to the Al-Aqsa channel that her mother alternated between; that and Saudi Arabia. Her mama didn't need the volume. She liked to see the streets of Jerusalem and Al-Aqsa Mosque. She liked to be able to roam the courtyards of the Noble Sanctuary even though she was in her bed. 'When I am better, Khadija, I want us to go there.'

Khadija noticed her mother's eyes light up whenever she spoke of Jerusalem, as though the land was full of her happiness, like she had left it behind at some point in her life. As though it belonged to her.

'To Al-Aqsa? I will take you.'

'When I'm better though and it is not too far, Khadija, not for all the benefits of praying there. May Allah grant us that. I miss it so much.'

'I didn't know you had been before, mama?'

She shifted in her bed slightly. 'Yes, many years ago. Before you were here. We used to live near there.'

'Who is "we"?' Khadija wondered if she would tell her more now. If she would talk about their family, or maybe mention a father at any stage. She thought she had to have one… hadn't she?

Her mother didn't answer, only stared at the TV and rubbed Khadija's hand with her trembling fingers. Khadija left her, the silence of her past becoming unbearable, so she turned on the tap, filled the kettle and stood listening to the heightening pitch of the kettle as it screamed to a boil. Her feet stood on the bare spot of the floor, warmed by where her mother had been. Khadija felt guilty for trying to push her secrets out into the open after she was responsible for her fall. She had left her on the floor for God knows how long and she thought she had the right to drag up all those memories of Jerusalem. She knew that Deir Yassin was near Jerusalem. She had heard about the atrocities there throughout her short life and she had no right to make her mother return to that place. Khadija couldn't shake the thought that by the time she would graduate and be the doctor she needed, it might be too late for her mother and all those that had passed before her.

Before she slept, she thought of Saladin. Tomorrow at school, she must thank him. For both the playground and tonight. But then she wondered how she could ever leave her mother alone again.

That evening, when her mother had fallen asleep, Khadija went to the rooftop and waited for the voice to begin …

Do you see what is behind the hilltops? No, you have never seen, so the monsters make up your nightmares and lay in wait for the cracks in your prayers so they can sneak in and rob you of your future as well as your dreams. Do you remember the stories of Deir Yassin? You can see what happened there in the town that they've tried to scrub from the maps, but the Nakba will not be scrubbed from our memories just as the soils cannot be stripped of their goodness. You didn't notice that before the hilltops, there are vast pasture lands that used to be farmed and fertile back in those glorious days before they came. You wonder how the land produces so much when the sunlight seems to skim over us, leaving us in the shadows. But there is something bigger. We are hidden here far above the sea, but the angels move the wind across the world, they rescue those who call to Allah on their desert journeys when they are about to be overcome by a murderous sword. These are stories that we tell to remind you. You have inherited much, not just the stories of your past. There is a future with you. Do not lose hope, Children of Palestine. We are not alone, Children of Palestine. We are soldiers of this land and this is where we belong.

Chapter 8

THE SUMMER EVENINGS BEGAN to be replaced by the colder nights of autumn. Her mother began to struggle more. The cold found its way into her bones and seized them up. Her fingers became painful to uncurl. Of course, Salma never said it out loud but Khadija could tell by the slight contortion in her face as she tried to move her body out of bed in the morning. 'Stop, Khadija *habibte*. Stop.'

'But it's *fajr*, mama.'

'I know, I know, but please leave my legs in the bed. I can pray here. That is the blessing of our Lord.' She said the words sincerely but Khadija noticed she turned her face slightly away from her as a tear slid down her cheek.

Khadija went to the door with her bag swung on her shoulder. She stood calmly at the door but her stomach, her heart, every organ in her body was tugging at her insides. She knew she should stay. But she knew by not going, her dreams were falling further and further away. The rain hit against the house, hard and heavy. Khadija turned around and dropped her bag in the hallway and stayed home. She knew that this was the start of the colder months and it probably wouldn't get easier until spring.

The days passed quickly. They became days of back-to-back care. When they needed food or medicine, Khadija would go into town. That was the part she enjoyed the most. She loved roaming around the streets, listening to the sounds of life. Market traders called out their prices, women checked fruit with young children in tow, trying the produce as they went, screaming out for the plastic toys that had been in the shops for weeks. Khadija had saved most of her mother's dress-making proceeds from Ramallah so the money was helping them through but with no new dresses, she wasn't sure how it was going to continue to buy food and pay for the pain relief her mother needed. She went to the fashion stalls to see if she could find anything that she could buy cheaply and then perhaps sell. But they were empty of any traditional embroidery; instead, they were packed with off-the-shelf clothes she had seen hundreds of times before. She had to learn how to sew or make some kind of income soon. She was flicking through the racks when she stopped. A dusky pink winter coat with a white faux fur trim swung on the rail. She picked it up, took off her thin sheet of a coat and slipped the new pink coat on. She glanced in the mirror in front and felt like a different person. How she would love that coat! She popped a couple of buttons closed and felt the luxurious, soft fabric wrapped around her.

'One hundred sheikal.'

Khadija turned around to see a teenage boy standing there with his hand out. 'For the coat.'

'Oh, I am not buying it. It … it doesn't fit.'

He gestured for her to hang it back up and turned around, uninterested.

She hung it back on the rail, looking at it and then feeling the notes and coins in her pockets. She had enough if he would accept a cheaper price and they almost always did, but the money had to last her for weeks. She did need a decent coat. No, she couldn't, she thought, walking off, still playing with the money in her pocket, wondering if maybe she could.

She thought about it on the way to the pharmacist so she could see how much her mother's medicine was. She handed the pharmacist a piece of paper with the name on it and she went around the back to check. When she came back, she handed it over with the price. 'Seventy sheikal in total.'

Khadija's cheeks flushed as she counted out the fund for the medicine. It came up short.

'I'm sorry, is that ok?'

She had some money in her other pocket but it had to last for food. She was sure the medicine was cheaper last time. She went to check her coat pockets and realised she wasn't wearing it. Her coat! She had left it behind at the stall. 'I'm sorry, I don't have any more on me.'

The pharmacist nodded and pulled out a ledger book full of owed monies and went back to her paperwork behind the desk. She thanked her again as she left the pharmacy, unsure of what the time was and concerned that the sky had already begun to grey as the cold, shorter evenings signalled that autumn was slipping into winter. She felt cold. By the time she had got back to the stall, her coat was gone.

'Excuse me, I left a coat here on the rails when I was trying one on,' she said to the boy that had spoken to her earlier. He didn't even respond; he just shrugged his shoulders as though he had never seen her before. She scoured the rails but it wasn't there.

She gave up and walked home. It was her fault for even trying the new one, she thought. That would teach her to be so ungrateful next time. She looked out to the rolling fields that fell behind the houses. There were no deer in them this year. Just as there weren't any during the year before that. She passed the familiar houses and could name every one of the families that lived in them. As she approached home, she saw the thick brick wall that cut through the back of her house. She opened the front door. They seldom locked them in the day-time. Strangers and tourists were unlikely to find themselves in these northern towns. The ones that dared to wander past the 'Danger' signs posted along the roads, rarely made it this far into the village before turning back. The only thing Khadija had to worry about was when the army tanks rolled through. But looking at the house from the street, it morphed into the ruins of its past and it looked so inhabitable that they would probably bypass it anyway. At least that's what Khadija had always hoped. That in some way, it was protected by its humble disintegrating form. That any humans already living in such a place couldn't be forced to live anywhere else and that they had absolutely no choice left but to stay. It was probably the lack of men in their house too. It was the young ones they wanted now, she heard. All she had to do was have faith. If the power of *dua* was as strong as the stories she heard, she knew it had no boundaries. Not even there.

With her thoughts renewed, under the darkening sky she ran in from the courtyard and prepared a dinner of broad beans in a creamy yoghurt sauce with a quarter packet of mince they had saved. Salma couldn't hold the spoon, so Khadija stepped in. As she went through the evening motions, her mind wandered to the school classroom. Would she be in trouble for missing more school? Could she catch up? What did they study today? Tomorrow was a different day. She still held hope that tomorrow would be different. She would be back in the four walls of the classroom learning again. Her mind expanding, her eyes glancing at the globe and everywhere in the world she could go to when she was free.

Just after the dawn prayer, there was a knock at the door. A timid knock, one Khadija was used to hearing. She rushed to let Amina in and was grateful to see her friendly face.

'I heard you have missed a couple of weeks of school?'

Khadija shrugged. It was probably more than that, she thought.

'You should have come and called me. You can't take everything on yourself. What about your school work?'

'I was hoping I could catch up.'

'Well, grab your bags and get to school then. If you hurry, you might not be late!'

Khadija was so relieved she threw her arms around her neck and she left quickly, grabbing a piece of bread on the side as she hadn't yet had breakfast. Outside, the wind sliced through the open fields. She fought against it and arrived at school, rushing to take her place in the classroom.

'I didn't think you came here anymore,' Aliya laughed.

Just as Khadija was about to respond, she noticed something on the back of Aliya's chair. A white-lined fur trim on a brand new dusky pink coat. Her heart sank. Of course Aliya would steal her dream coat.

Miss Ayesha came in and Khadija noticed a surprised look on her face that changed to a smile on seeing her in the classroom. Suddenly, Khadija felt better. She brushed thoughts of the brand new coat aside and began to study.

When Khadija returned home, the house glowed with warm lights from inside and she could hear the mellow sound of voices and laughter and the smell of food wafting out of the gate, permeating the cold air. She couldn't imagine a sweeter home to come back to. Amina and Salma had always been the best of friends for as long as Khadija could remember. There were weeks when they didn't see her as she had family in Jericho and she would travel there, especially in the winters. Any of the families that could, would migrate to its mild climate and return to their hillside houses in the summer when Jericho became too hot.

Khadija walked into a scene with them sitting together and a hot fire burning in the grate. A fire Khadija hadn't managed to light since last year. Her mum was in her prayer shawl with a new heavy fleece blanket wrapped around her. 'Do you like my new socks?' Salma said, laughing as she rolled up her prayer shawl to show Khadija her thick socks animated with a badly sewn reindeer on them. Amina began laughing with them and Khadija smiled because Amina was there to help. To help make her mother happy, to make the stark walls feel like a home and because in a long time, she hadn't heard laughter inside it.

The days passed happily as the winter descended around them. Sometimes when Khadija would return from school, Amina would be taking her mother for a short walk and a shot of fresh air around the courtyard, taking her to the bottom near the wall where you could just see the fields beyond the ruins. She watched as her mother glanced up to the night-time sky she hadn't seen in so long, only to see her turn to the left and almost fall down as though a great weight landed on her shoulders from up above. Amina saw it too and immediately returned her to the house where her sobs, although muffled under the bedclothes, could be heard through the thin walls.

Khadija wondered what could have made her sad. She thought she knew everything there was to know about her but there were some secrets she knew her mother would never tell a child. As if when the adults spoke of raids and kidnappings in the night from the army, of boys and young men left to rot inside jail cells, was kept from the children by these women and mothers who carried on cooking and cleaning and hoping. But it was back, that thumping in Khadija's heart. The image of the army base above the hilltops. The sound of the trucks passing through in the dead of night. It was always there, etching itself into her subconscious. She even had nightmares that she had been there at a raid before. That she had hidden but seen it all. It was impossible, she told herself. But the stories were real. And from when she was as young as she could remember, they had spoken about them in whispers. Whispers that could be heard through the walls. Tears that could be heard through muffled clothes. Eyes that could peer through the cracks as houses lit up and screams echoed down the streets. Generations of stories etching into her heart.

Khadija knew that even though she hadn't been part of it, she was born Palestinian so she was already born with their scars. Her heart beat harder underneath her skin and she closed her eyes tightly. She tried to fall asleep, imagining the day she could take out all the pain from people's hearts and replace them with shiny new ones that knew nothing of their past. Her heart beat with the rotation of the lights spinning from the hilltops.

Chapter 9

THE YEARS PASSED SWIFTLY from harvest to harvest, from Ramadan to Eid. The sun had risen each morning; the moon had continued to pursue its own orbit. Her friends became older, as did she. As did her mother. Khadija settled into a calm existence of hard days and long nights. Her childhood before the attack was a distant memory that sometimes filtered into the rooms, or out onto the fields when she used to reminisce about her long summer days. Sometimes a scent in the air would remind her the cherries were sweetened and ripe for picking or the apricots, like balls of sunshine, were falling off the trees. But her world wasn't an exploration of the outdoors. It was stuck in textbooks and classrooms and the smells of her summer were of chalk, blackboards and books. As often happens with normality, the routine and responsibilities take over and fill every ounce of time, leaving nothing left. They had scraped by with enough food to live and that was her life between those walls that they had made a home. It was the nature of life that this would shortly change too, although Khadija hadn't expected it. She returned from school on an ordinary afternoon, expecting an ordinary evening, but stopped dead in the courtyard. The light across the fields had sunk. The house, despite emanating voices from inside, seemed silent. Khadija could hear their voices through the door that was left slightly ajar.

'She doesn't even know yet,' the voice said.

Khadija thought back to that morning. Had it been a normal morning? Yes, it had, she reminisced. Her brain searched for the moments before she left. She had left her mother in bed as she packed her school bag. Her mother's voice called for her, 'Khadija, I need you to come here for a minute.'

'I can't, mama, I am late already.'

'Please, *habibte*, just for a minute.'

Khadija remembered she felt distracted with her upcoming exams and this morning she had been running late, so as she went over to her mother and sat next to her, cupping her soft hand in hers, she wondered if her face exposed her impatience.

'I need to tell you something.'

'Yes, mama. Can we please talk about it later? I have an exam and I am already finding it hard to catch up after–' Khadija stopped talking.

Her mother let go of her hand and Khadija thought she registered some hurt on her face but couldn't be sure of where it stemmed from.

'Yes, you go, *habibte*. We can talk about it later.'

Khadija kissed her hand. 'After school, I will come straight home and you can tell me then,' Khadija said, closing the door.

She couldn't even remember if she had said *salam*, or told her that she loved her. All of a sudden that seemed to matter now. Had she said it? She must have said she loved her, she said it every time she left.

Khadija only stopped rerunning the events through her head when she heard Amina sobbing. She knew her voice well and it was broken through the tears. Khadija's heart sunk.

'Please let me tell her,' Amina's voice said.

'She will find out after school, by me. I am her guardian now.'

Khadija didn't dare walk in. She didn't want to face what or who was behind the door. She looked behind her to run. But where could she go? She had no choice but to walk forward. Those steps she took every day, one foot in front of the other, the short distance from where she was stood to the door felt like an eternity. Her heart was beating quickly, she felt nauseous.

She pushed open the door to Amina seated on the sofa, with a tissue in her hand that she was uncurling and staring at, and her uncle who was standing with his hands in his pockets and an expression on his face that Khadija couldn't read. He seemed to be thinking about something as his eyes looked out the window.

'What's happened?' Khadija said, as she searched around the rooms whilst they looked on. 'Where is mama?' she said, coming back in after realising it seemed foolish to search the tiny house for her mother who quite obviously wasn't there. Khadija knew by the atmosphere, she knew by the house's emptiness and the flickering sadness she was trying to subdue in her chest, she knew that her mother wasn't with them.

Khadija turned to Amina. 'Where is she?'

Amina snapped out of her daze and began to sob again. She clasped Khadija's hands and beckoned for her to sit on the sofa next to her. 'We had to rush her to the hospital, Khadija. I'm so sorry, dear.'

'Did she need another operation?' Khadija said, standing up and reaching for her bag. 'I don't need to go to school, I can go to the hospital now. Will you take me, Amina, please?'

'Shush, dear, sit down.'

'No, you don't understand. I need to speak to her.' Khadija tried to show Amina how important it was that she spoke to her without her uncle realising. She knew he couldn't be trusted, so Khadija whispered, 'She had something she wanted to tell me.'

'I understand, dear, but you have to sit down, you have to listen to what I am trying to tell you.'

'She is dead! Ok? Do you understand now? She can't speak to you, she can't speak to anyone,' her uncle spat out.

'Jahid, please. She is just a child.'

Her uncle stormed out of the house, waving his hand behind him as if to give up on them both and left the door wide open. The house seemed to exhale once he had left.

Khadija was sobbing on Amina as she spoke to her. 'I'm sorry, dear. I wanted to tell you gently. She didn't make it. Her heart, it stopped beating, there was nothing we could do. She is with the angels now; they will be taking her to her place in paradise.'

Khadija was crying more because she held the secret of her last moments with her. She couldn't imagine that she would leave her in the morning and not know if she had even said *salam* or I love you. What were her last words? She would never be there for her to talk to. Her voice would never recite to her in the early hours of the morning. Khadija was alone.

The afternoon passed in the cloud of her own thoughts as she repeatedly rejected offers of food or tea to help her body recover from the shock. Amina left her with repeated reminders that she wouldn't be long and she insisted that she would be back to stay with her once she had collected her things. She tucked her up in bed, urging her to sleep and Khadija heard the door lock behind her as she left. She must have had her mother's key. The bed felt warm as though she had just been there a moment ago. She closed her eyes and could still hear her voice reciting the Quran. She didn't know how to sleep alone. She didn't know how there was life without her. She switched on the TV to dull out the deafening silence and fill it with the sound of her mother's favourite channel, Al-Aqsa TV. They had never made it there together. There were many things they were robbed of doing together. They were even robbed of their life together. Khadija could not hold it in any longer. If she was in any state to think, she would have been relieved that the only ones close enough to hear her cries and screams were the dead next door.

***

Amina managed to rouse her for the burial. It was swiftly after her death, as was the tradition in Islam. The burial was next door. It passed in a blur of black tears and prayers for a paradise that lay above the skies.

That night she wanted to be alone. She couldn't rest in the bed. It was too empty. She took her childhood blanket and crept out of the room as if her mother might still wake up. Out on the rooftop, she glanced up to the sky but it was a canvas of black with barely any glow of light.

Look, Khadija, the lights are spinning on the hilltops. They are looking for you. All these years and they haven't found you yet.

Listen, Khadija, can you hear? The night the raids begin. Listen, Khadija, can you hear the door banging? It is an angel disguised as a beggar woman, who is desperate for food. Or wait, it isn't just one. It is another group of Palestinian women. Their men are gone, their gardens and their homes have been snatched alongside their children. Look what they bring to you, Khadija. Just their stories and the dresses on their backs that no longer fit. They are seeking shelter for the night and beyond. Go and open the door, Khadija, do not leave them abandoned at your door.

It isn't the angels, Khadija, it is the monsters playing tricks on you as they shift shapes in the night. You can see, Khadija, because you are a heart doctor, remember? You can cut open the chests of birds and peer inside them. Did you find what you were looking for, Khadija? Use that vision to see past these monsters at your door. You can see that their hearts are black so do not answer. Do not let them into your heart.

During her nightmares it was her mother's voice, speaking in rhymes and secrets, that Khadija was so terrified of. She ran inside and slammed the door. She bolted the chain and sat in the corner of the room watching the square window alternate between darkness and light.

***

Khadija could hear the voices coming from inside the door. She listened outside.

'So, as you know, despite her frugal living, she has left the girl this property which the lawyer has rightly informed me includes the garden.'

Khadija thought of the small slice of garden that wrapped around the front of the property.

'And whoever takes care of the girl gains possession of it. Because of course, it costs money to raise a child. A girl not quite completed her education. An awful lot of money,' he seemed to be muttering the last bit. 'We all know what would happen if, Allah forbid, she was left without a guardian.'

The room fell silent. No one argued with that. Khadija herself wondered. She recognised Amina's voice. 'But it isn't right, that a young girl will be living without–'

'Hush, Amina. Why are you even here?'

Khadija listened to the voice of the man she could hear. She recognised it. It took a few moments to sink in. It was her uncle.

'I am only saying, she won't have a–'

Khadija heard a chair move, the leg scraping against the floor.

'Get out! You aren't welcome here,' her uncle's voice broke. Her grieving tones became a shriek.

Khadija darted out the way of the door.

'I'm sorry, dear. I tried to keep you but I am not your family. In this instance you are to be cared for by Jahid,' Amina said, almost knocking into Khadija as she fled the house. 'Before I go, come quickly, there is something I must tell you. Outside. By the gate.'

Khadija pushed her feet into her sandals and clumsily tripped after her.

'What is it, Amina?'

'Your mother, she–'

'Khadija, get back here now,' another voice shouted from the house.

Amina looked up, her face pale in the cold light.

'Khadija, get back here now.'

'I'm sorry, dear. May Allah protect you.'

Khadija watched her running down the street, her faded *abaya* trailing after her like a ghost.

Chapter 10

SHE FOLLOWED HER UNCLE out of the house, taking with her the bag of belongings she owned and a few keepsakes from her mum. All it amounted to was a bar of her favourite soap that smelt like her, the fleece blanket she wore, her books and a bunch of keys that she had kept locked in her bedside table since Khadija could remember. She followed her uncle out onto the street and watched as he locked up the house. Khadija kept glancing back at it in the dark, its low profile almost disappearing into the earth.

They climbed into his car and drove through the streets until they arrived at a gate that was locked shut. It was a house in the neighbourhood, occupying the corner plot at the end. It was too dark to see what lay past it but there were no more houses there. Even through the darkness, she could make out the house was at least three storeys high. It was one of the older, traditional houses with columns at the front and arched windows, almost triple the size of the window holes in the walls at her home. The garden was tangled and overgrown. Climbers clambered up the wall. The heavy door opened with a creak, opening up to a wide stairwell reaching out and splitting off into two directions upstairs. The door closed behind them with a bang, disturbing old leaves and cobwebs that blew in the air.

The hallway was dark but from what Khadija could see, the portraits of faces hanging on the wall, unusual figurines cluttered the tables with distorted shapes of animals and creatures she had never seen before. He must have collected them on his travels, Khadija thought.

'Don't for one second think that because I have this place, that I am rich. I am not,' her uncle said.

'This is where you live now. She may have wanted us all to think she was a pauper but she must have had something.'

'She has a bill at the pharmacy. She couldn't often buy food. She–'

'Stop blathering, child. You will stay as long as is necessary then you must find your own way in this world. Like we all do.'

Khadija followed him as he walked up the staircase and pointed to a small room at the far end of the corridor.

'That's where you stay. You can continue to go to school for now.'

Khadija nodded, although she had no idea what he was saying, being taken to this new house, away from the only comfort she had known which was to live amongst her mother's memories, things and spaces that they used to share together.

'And never cross the landing into my side of the house. It is out of bounds. Do you understand?'

Khadija nodded again.

He slapped her across the face. 'Talk, you aren't a mute.'

'I won't go in there,' she said. Through the stinging burn left by his handprint, Khadija gritted her teeth and vowed to never forget it.

'No, you will not. Because if you do, you will be out on the streets and no one is going to care about another orphan.'

Khadija lay down in the wooden bed in the room. Its mattress was hard and there was only a thin scrap of cotton over it, so she unrolled the fleece blanket Amina had given to her mother and wrapped it around her. It smelt of home.

Inside the room, she heard knocking noises from above the ceiling. Her feet made the wood beneath her feet creak as she walked along it. A whip of cold air sliced through the room when she pulled back the old curtains. The curtains looked as though they had been expensive once. The material was heavy between her fingers and the borders were handsewn. The wardrobe splintered as she opened it. A layer of dust smudged beneath where her fingers were. There was nothing inside.

As she lay there listening to the wind howl outside the window, she was reminded of a similar night when she had curled up with her mother, maybe five years or so ago. It was one of the earliest memories she had of the storyteller.

Don't turn your houses into graveyards, because they are for the dead and the dead do not belong with the living. You can't see the jinn but they live amongst us. They inhabit our houses and when they have been left unattended, they fill the spaces and when you walk in, they watch you. They hide underneath the beds. They hide in the empty wardrobes and they watch you as you sleep. Don't turn your houses into graveyards, recite Quran in them. The devils run away if they hear Allah's words. Pray in the rooms, let the light in so you can see properly and don't sleep until you have prayed. Protect yourself from the evil that lies around you. Waiting. Turn your homes into those where the living belong.

Khadija closed her eyes and began to read Quran until she fell asleep.

The next morning, Khadija awoke early. She washed in the basin in her room using her mother's soap. It had shrunk since she had taken it from her mother's bedside dresser. She patted it dry with a towel and left it on her pillow to preserve it. She opened the curtains onto the front garden outside that led to an empty street. There were no houses opposite. Just a thicket of cypress trees that had grown unattended for years. The other houses began further up the road towards the village. She tiptoed downstairs. Dusty piles of paperwork, old newspapers and magazines were left on a side table in the hall. The artwork on the walls was of old Palestinian maps, detailed with towns that used to exist. Street names, family names. The different areas were drawn in different styles by different artists, documenting and preserving what was being eroded. Khadija spent some time tracing her finger along from the main towns of Jerusalem, Ramallah and Jericho. She could see the outline of the coast and Gaza. It wasn't something she expected to see in this gloomy house.

Next to the hallway was a smaller room; a study, she thought. Its shelves were full of books. A desk sat in the middle, facing out towards a window that overlooked the street she guessed, but she couldn't see because of the closed curtains.

She opened the front door and peered out onto the street. She wasn't sure what she was looking for, but somehow, she expected the world to look different. To have changed because hers had changed so abruptly. But of course, the street was unchanged. A mistlike warm breath hung in the air and shrouded the view. She stepped out and knocked something on the step. She panicked and held her breath, hoping her uncle hadn't heard. She looked down and there was a tin with a note, *For*

Khadija. She stuffed it under her top and ran back upstairs to her bedroom. Just as she was about to open the mystery box, she heard her uncle's footsteps approaching before the door swung open. Khadija hid the package behind her back.

'What have you got there?'

'Nothing,' Khadija said, instantly regretting her lack of a better response as her uncle reached behind her back and grabbed it out of her hands. 'It was left outside. It is for me.'

'I will take this,' he said, waving it just out of reach in front of her face.

Khadija went to snatch it back but he moved it and smirked. She was going to argue with him, but she could tell by his face there was no point. If he realised he had upset her, he would just relish in this moment of power even more. 'I will ask Amina then. It must be from her.'

'She isn't here anymore.'

'Why? Why has she left?'

Her uncle didn't respond. He just smiled and walked off.

She hurried down the stairs to the kitchen as he left to go to his side of the house, disappearing into his bedroom. She ran her hand along the hand-carved wooden units mounted on the walls in a U-shape, stopping at a sink positioned below a window. She peered out to a brick wall that seemed to cut through the back of the house where you would expect its garden to be.

Next to the sink, a grand, glass-fronted cabinet was stacked with plates, crockery, different types of coffee cups and tea sets. Khadija imagined that at one point its curtains would have been wide open, its lawn full of visitors, the fine crockery taken out and used on summer days. She imagined setting it up with the front doors unlocked, and the sound of voices and laughter in the light spring breeze with the taste of mint and homemade Arabic sweets in the air.

'Daydreaming again, I see? Off in the land of the others, are you?'

Khadija refocused and saw her uncle standing at the entranceway to the kitchen, his bulky figure blocking out the light from the hall.

'*Salam,* uncle,' she answered automatically, embarrassed that he had been watching her.

He muttered something inaudible and adjusted his trousers which seemed to be drooping underneath the weight of his stomach. 'Get yourself off to school then,' he said shortly.

Khadija didn't say anything. For some reason, she hadn't thought of school. She had been so consumed by the absence of her mother that she had forgotten about the ordinary. She thought of the classroom, of Aliya. Of what they would say.

'Go on then, what are you waiting for? Go.'

Ahead of her on the street, she saw someone walking and knew immediately it was Saladin. She could recognise his walk anywhere. She followed him, watching his slow and purposeful steps. She smiled at his consistency. She crossed over the road and fell into a shallow puddle, gasping as the water soaked through her socks.

He turned around. She pretended not to notice.

'Khadija?'

'Oh, Saladin, I didn't see you there.'

'That's strange. You were behind me for quite a while,' he said with a knowing smile, that Khadija couldn't help feeling happy that she had seen.

'To Allah we belong and to Allah we return.'

'Yes. You were at the burial?'

Saladin nodded.

'Sorry, I didn't say much–'

'I didn't expect you to,' Saladin said. 'How was it leaving your home behind?'

'I miss it already and it has only been one night,' Khadija said, as they walked towards the part of the village closer to her old home. She didn't want to be reminded now, so she changed the subject. 'How is school going?'

'Yes, the same. Exams coming up soon.'

'Have you decided what you are doing after?'

'Not yet. You still on track to be a heart doctor?'

Khadija nodded. 'Yes, I think so.'

But as she said it, she panicked. Did she want to do it now? Her mother had already passed away. She could no longer help her. She would never have been able to afford it but without her mother's support, with her uncle so difficult, it might be completely out of reach now. The thoughts swamped her mind until they arrived at school.

In the playground, she heard a voice. It repeated itself. 'I said, living with Jahid. He hasn't been around for ages. Don't you ever wonder where he has been?'

Khadija didn't like to answer Aliya. Aliya rarely asked a question without having an ulterior motive.

'I heard baba talking and well, the house has been left empty for so long, we wondered why the Israelis hadn't taken it.'

'I don't know anything about him.'

'No, no one does. Strange, isn't it?'

Khadija shrugged her shoulders.

'You have to wonder, don't you? When people leave and everything stays the same.'

'Aliya. Don't be disrespectful,' Saladin said. It seemed to shut her up.

But Khadija knew none of this.

'I suppose you wouldn't know, would you, Khadija, because–'

'Aliya, just give it a rest. We are all on the same side.'

'Unless you're a spy.'

'You watch too many American films.'

'I bet you two won't come,' Aliya said, swinging her legs down over the side of the climbing frame.

Khadija turned around and noticed her face smirking at her.

'Where?' Khadija asked, tentatively.

'We are going to the graveyard tonight.'

'Why?' Khadija asked, but inside she was reminded of something, something about the place had stirred a memory somewhere in the recesses of her brain.

'What do you mean, why? Haven't you heard the stories about the spies that gather there at night?' She jumped down. 'Oh, of course you haven't, you've been too busy moving house and getting rich in the process.'

Khadija lunged forward and pushed her. Saladin pulled her back. 'She isn't worth it, just leave it. That's what she wants.'

'Well, whilst we are out doing our journalism and getting famous from what we film, you two will probably be inside being good. Just like you're told.'

Khadija was sure Aliya would have more TV channels and probably knew more about these things than she did. Sometimes

on the news channels, she saw people from Palestine being in-
terviewed and Khadija wondered if people all around the world
would see you and you would become famous. She wondered
if going there would reveal something new? Then she thought
of her uncle too. Maybe the rumours were true. What if he was
a spy and she was the one who discovered it? She could imagine
him sneaking about at night in a place like that.

'Count me in.'

Saladin shook his head and whispered in her ear, 'Khadija,
no. You don't want to do this. It won't lead to anything good.'

It was too late. Khadija had made up her mind.

'There aren't any spies around here. It's just made-up stories
that you are falling for.'

'How would you know, Sheikh boy? No one would tell you
anything.'

Saladin turned to Khadija. 'Don't go. It's too dangerous.
You know the graveyard is right underneath the army encamp-
ment at the top of the hill.'

'That's it, listen to the Sheikh's son. He couldn't possibly
go. Maybe he will "see" things like he did last time.' Aliya started laughing.

Saladin's cheeks turned red. Khadija knew she was talking
about the last trip they went on with school, one of the days
she had missed, but she hadn't missed them talking about it.
'He felt the earth shake,' they laughed. Khadija heard he refused to go inside the church. It didn't surprise her; he was
connected to this world in a way she understood.

She changed the subject, 'Oh, be quiet, Aliya. You wouldn't
go without us anyway because you would be worried about
getting your precious hands dirty.' She heard the others laugh

from behind their hands. 'He will come. He will come with me.'

It wasn't exactly what she was intending to say, and she wasn't sure it was even true. But it stopped Aliya from questioning him anymore and they left them behind. Saladin and Khadija sat in silence for a few moments. Her mind wandered to the graveyard. She felt sick to her stomach.

***

She arrived home mortified and covered in dirt. She had uncovered nothing except her own foolishness. That was what Aliya had planned to do all along. She would never fall for her tricks again. She was no closer to discovering the truth about her uncle either. Aliya knew nothing. Instead, Khadija would discover what he was hiding.

Although she only lived in a few rooms of her uncle's house, there were many she hadn't been in. Like a stranger inhabiting its halls, it was mostly out of bounds. So, when her uncle had gone out and she was left alone, the first thing she did was to dig out the old keys and unlock the doors that he kept so private. She was sure the parcel that was left for her would be somewhere in the house too. This could be her chance to find out what it was and who had left it for her. She tried a few keys in the lock that separated his half of the house, until with a satisfying click, the door opened and led down a hallway of its own with doors leading off of it. She unlocked the first door inside the hallway which opened with a loud creak as though it had been left undisturbed for years. She opened the curtains to a stream of dust particles floating in the room. She sneezed. The sound echoed around the empty part of the house, ricocheting off the walls. She stopped. Silence resumed. In the room was a large, wooden desk, piled high with old paperwork. A floor to ceiling high built-in bookshelf covered the left-hand wall. Everything was covered in dust. She walked over to the table and saw it was covered with black and white photographs. She flicked through them. Scenes of war. Of tanks rolling through the villages. Of razed houses with families stood outside. Dates and names written on the backs of them. Familiar names she had heard before. Names that had accompanied the stories. She turned over to a new pile and at the top was a black and white image of a gate. It was a wrought iron gate built into a brick wall. She stared at the image. She had seen the gate before; there was one like it near her old home. Underneath the photo of the gate was a large garden. It was full of greenery, grapes and orchards. A barefoot woman harvested it, with a basket in her hand and a small child on her hip. She put it to one side. Piles of old newspapers lay stacked high. Records of events, of time passing, it was the narrative of her homeland. She took the picture of the gate and closed the curtain and then locked the door behind her.

Out in the hallway, the corridor stretched before her. She wondered why her uncle was so adamant that she shouldn't be in those rooms, when there wasn't anything that she hadn't seen or heard before. Maybe Aliya was right. Could he have been a spy? Is that why he had all this archived away in a locked room? She thought Aliya was just being Aliya until she remembered her neighbours visiting her mother when he had left. They were saying how he shouldn't leave the house because empty houses were taken over, especially one at the end of the village with its size and position.

Khadija's mother had always refused to comment and said that it should be locked and left in the hands of Allah whilst he travelled. She explained the soldiers of Palestine would be taken care of by Allah. That's all she had said on it. Now Khadija was there she wondered if he had defected to the other side. She wondered if that was the reason for his moods. If he had sold his soul to the devil and in return had kept his life. She continued unlocking doors and rummaging around in the depths of his history but it revealed nothing, except for the empty beds of children who must have been dreamt of at some point. She imagined what the house would have been like if it was full of children and a wife. If there would have been dinners and parties during the Eid celebrations that passed as the years went by. If they would have made a treehouse in the old tree on the front of the street. If they would have been happy in a house like this one. She was careful to lock all the doors behind her and only remove the pictures of the gate and the gardens. They held a strange appeal and the gate looked like one near her old house. Could it be the same one? Khadija thought she would discover where it was and find out why he had a photograph of it locked away. He was hiding more from her, she just knew it. There was a reason she recognised this and he had hidden it from her.

Khadija knew she couldn't go around waving the photograph in front of people because it would get back to her uncle and then he would know her secret. So, she took it down to Saladin just after the prayer had finished. She waited for him outside the mosque.

'Don't tell anyone, Saladin, but do you know where this is?'

He looked at the picture, then looked back at Khadija. 'Where did you get this from?'

'Does it matter?'

Saladin frowned. 'Well, yes, you shouldn't be going around trying to uncover things that are meant to be kept hidden.'

'Do you know where it is or not?'

'Even if I did, I wouldn't tell you.'

'Well, I am going off to discover it. I am sure it means something to me. Do you want to come with me?' Khadija folded her lips in as though it was the only way for her to stop talking to try and convince him. Instead, she just asked him again, 'Are you coming?'

Khadija knew he would because there wasn't a lot to keep them entertained during the summer. The weather was also warm and light enough for them to be out for a good few hours. The grown-ups were busy in their gardens, inviting their neighbours and preparing the late afternoon meals where they would barbecue whatever meat, chicken or fish was going at the markets that day. The air smelt of singed smoke and the younger children were out in the gardens and swinging from trees, throwing cherries at them as they passed. Khadija relished the independence of not being confined to her gardens and laughed as she ran past and dodged their attempts. They walked past the mosques and houses until they hit the fields approaching the house where Khadija used to live. She stopped outside a mass of tangled leaves and branches climbing over the wall.

'I have seen it before, I am sure of it,' Khadija said, pulling at the leaves, 'Are you going to help me?'

Saladin reluctantly began helping her, revealing the gate in the photograph. 'I knew I had seen it here! But not for years, it is so overgrown,' Khadija said, trying with all her strength to untwist the wrought-iron handle.

'It is locked and probably rusted shut. You will never be able to open it,' Saladin said. 'Fine. I will go in through the house and see if I can find a way.'

'Are you sure you want to go in?'

'Well, it is my house I guess.'

Saladin stayed back by the gate as she entered. 'Aren't you coming?'

'It doesn't feel right,' he murmured.

She glanced up the hilltops. There was no movement. No lights. She walked around the side of the house and peered in the windows. It looked different somehow now it was empty. After staying at her uncle's for so long it seemed smaller. The brick wall that extended out of the house ran down across where the gardens should be. She hadn't ever explored it much but now her mama wasn't around she had complete freedom to explore.

Saladin had silently come to her side and was tugging her shirt. 'Khadija, it's too close. You've had your fun now, let's go.'

'Get off me, Saladin. I want to find out what's behind this wall. Haven't you ever wondered? It's big enough to hide an entire house behind it.'

'It's too close to the hilltop.'

'It's the middle of the day. No one cares.'

Khadija couldn't get through the exterior wall. There were no breaks in it.

She tried to open the door to the house to see if she could get access inside but the door was locked and she didn't have the key. So, she went to the side and threw a brick through the window above the door.

'Khadija!'

She ignored Saladin's shout and climbed through, careful not to catch her wrist on the broken glass as she opened the handle from inside. Inside, it was empty and cool as the sunlight barely had any way of penetrating the thick stone walls or the small windows. She shivered. The wall that used to be her living room wall was smashed open. Broken plaster and dust littered the room. The tapestry that hung on the wall was on the floor; it had been ripped off. She approached the hole in the wall and found it didn't lead to an open space outside. She had heard of spaces inside walls where people had hidden before. Was this one of those secret spaces? Someone or something had smashed a hole into the wall that used to close in their living room. Khadija peered through to find it was a disused alleyway. Through the hole, about a metre in distance was the exterior brick wall that ran around the ruins. She climbed inside but it was too narrow to walk down and seemed closed in at each end as there was no natural light that filtered through. Was it a secret hiding place in the wall? Did the tapestry cover a secret entrance to a safe place? What or who were they hiding from? Had she got out just in time?

***

Back at home, she crept in the front door to find her uncle in the hallway.

'You made me jump. You're like some little *jinn*, creeping around—and what are you covered in?' he said, grabbing her arm and pulling her closer to inspect.

'I was just at the old quarry site.'

'Still a liar then,' he said smugly. 'Anyway, go and clean yourself up. I have someone who has come to meet you.'

Khadija ran upstairs to change, more eager to destroy the evidence that she had been home than to please her uncle and his guest.

When Khadija came back down the stairs, her uncle was there to greet her with an odd smile on his face. She knew something was wrong when he spoke. 'Come through to the lounge.'

His tone changed the moment he was in earshot of his guest. He had never welcomed her like this. It unnerved her. Who was it he was speaking like this to? She walked into the lounge, slowly. She wasn't sure if it was her footsteps hitting the floor or her heart thudding that created the methodical beat hitting through her body. She peered around the door. 'Don't act so shy, Khadija. He isn't going to bite.'

He. Khadija had only heard of one reason men came to visit the houses where there were unmarried girls present. She sat uncomfortably on the sofa, trying not to look at him. Trying not to breathe so that her body wouldn't give away her fear and helplessness.

'Now we know you have been getting yourself into trouble. And well, it's not befitting for a girl,' he glanced at the visitor, 'A young lady, to be acting in this way.'

'I am Mr Masood. You may have heard my name before?'

Khadija turned to face him as he spoke. He was a few years older than her uncle. He was wearing a brown faded suit. It clung to his body a bit too tightly. It made him shift uncomfortably in his seat as he tried to loosen the fabric. His glasses kept slipping down his nose, so instead, he lifted his head at an angle when he looked at her.

'Answer him, Khadija,' her uncle said, slipping back into the tone she was used to. 'He asked you a question.'

'No, I haven't.'

'Tell me a bit about what you would like to do when you are older?'

Khadija wasn't sure what to say. As if it was some kind of trap. But she had said it so often and to anyone who would listen that the words came out almost automatically.

'I want to be a doctor.'

'Big dreams,' he said, nodding. 'Expensive dreams.'

He seemed to look the other way, momentarily.

'I think it's best if I go now. I will let you two discuss what we spoke about and I will see you next week.' He turned to look at Khadija's uncle. 'I trust everything will be in order before I return?'

He stood up and nodded, whilst walking with him to the door.

Khadija ran upstairs and flung her clothes into a disused leather suitcase she had found in the bottom of a wardrobe. She was startled by a short laugh behind her. She turned to the doorway, where her uncle was standing.

'What are you going to do? Run away? Go on then. Be glad to be rid of you, little demon child. You wouldn't last a week on your own.'

Khadija looked at him through her tears and hated him with everything inside her. She hated him but she knew he was right. She ran over to the window, where the skies were darkening. The lights started appearing again on the hilltops. Powerful beams rotating round and round through the night. She turned around to face the room. The darkness was wrapped around her from all angles and she didn't know which one scared her the most. She noticed that when her uncle left, he had shut the door behind him. She ran over to the handle. She pulled at it with all her strength. He had locked her in. Her hands became damp, her hair clung to her forehead and fell in front of her face as she panicked, the four walls closing in on her. The room started to constrict her, her breathing became tight. She thought of the graveyard. It was her own undoing. She had dared to walk over the graves of those closed in under the earth. She remembered what the stories were. She remembered the storyteller. The storyteller told her they weren't resting. They could hear those footsteps above them but they couldn't walk with them. They couldn't go back on earth and pray one last time, or ask for forgiveness from their graves. They had to endure what they had sown. She thought of Saladin. How odd in that moment of fear that she thought of him. His voice. He had told her not to go. He had warned her that it would lead to nothing good. She might have stayed quiet when Aliya mocked him for seeing something, but she felt it too. The ghosts of their heritage were never far away. It was in the bullet holes of the houses; it was in the absence of the missing ones in the streets. It was in the stories that haunted them. It was in the graves of those who had gone.

Khadija must have fallen asleep breathless as she woke up abruptly with a start. It was still dark outside. She checked the time and knew she could make *fajr* prayer and catch Saladin at the mosque. She glanced at her door, remembering it was locked and was therefore surprised to find it ajar. Had she dreamt the whole thing? Had she even been locked in or just panicked? Why would her uncle bother locking her in when he allowed her to go to school every day? Khadija didn't waste any more time considering and left her room behind, heading straight to the mosque.

She was out of breath when she got there, but just caught Saladin as he was about to walk up the steps to the speaker for the *athan*.

'Saladin, wait!' she shouted.

He turned around with a startled look on his face. 'What are you doing here?'

'Hold on,' she said, 'before you call the *athan*,' pulling the T-shirt on his back to yank him away from the steps. 'Wait, Saladin, please. You have to help me.'

'What's happened?'

'Marry me.'

Saladin stopped talking. His cheeks flushed before he answered, 'What are you talking about?'

Her face must have given away that she wasn't joking. She was serious.

'What, why?'

'Uncle is planning on marrying me off to someone and I need a reason to go, I can't run away, I have nowhere to go and I know that if I had to get married, I would at least want someone my own age.'

'Slow down, we haven't even finished school.'

Saladin heard his father's voice call him from inside.

'Wait for me after,' he said, scampering up the stairs. Khadija heard him breathe deeply before calling the worshippers to prayer. As Saladin went inside, Khadija glanced around the street and saw some of the villagers switching the street lamps on and heading towards the mosque. She ran off before anyone could see her but all she could hear for the rest of the day was Saladin's voice in her head and a feeling inside that she should have stayed, at least to make her prayers. To have some sanctuary before the real world began again, when the day brightened up and people began moving in their houses.

A knock at the door interrupted her thoughts. Her uncle was out so she went downstairs to see who it was and opened the door to Saladin. Her face flushed.

'You left quickly after the prayers.'

'Yes, sorry.'

'Baba said it was a Mr Masood that came. He saw him in town before he arrived at yours. Why didn't you tell me his name before?'

'Why would it have made any difference?'

'Because your uncle isn't marrying you off. My baba told me. Mr Masood is Head of the Ministry of Education.'

Khadija didn't know what else to say. Her uncle eventually came home and found Khadija impatiently waiting for him on the stairs.

'Do you have something you need to tell me, uncle?' Khadija tried to tone down the irritation in her voice but she wasn't sure she was successful.

He took off his jacket and swung it over the bannister, almost hitting her head but she didn't move.

'Uncle!'

'Don't talk to me like that in my house,' he said, but then instantly reined his voice in.

Khadija wasn't sure why but she remained silent on the stairs, waiting to be told.

'You are always going on about being a doctor, so Mr Masood has arranged quite an opportunity. He is an old acquaintance of mine.'

'Why would you do this for me? It doesn't make any sense.'

He threw her a look of disapproval.

'It is in Doha, Qatar.'

Khadija let the last bit sink in. Qatar? She hadn't heard much about Qatar. She knew it was in the Arabian Gulf, a tiny island far away from home.

'I can't go to Qatar.'

'Why not?'

'On my own?'

'Well, I don't see why not if the school will have you.'

'How did I—but my grades aren't high enough to start medical school on a scholarship... I just don't understand any of this. Our graduation isn't far off.'

'You are under my guardianship. You are going to Doha and you will study there. There is nothing more to discuss. It has already been arranged.'

Khadija thought of her childhood role model, Iqbal Al Assad, who had graduated from high school at twelve years old and from medical school at twenty. But somehow it didn't seem right. Was she really unique enough to be awarded a scholarship? She highly doubted it. Khadija walked outside, spending a few moments letting the news sink in. It felt as if it was happening to someone else. Not her. Things like this didn't happen to Khadija.

She walked back to her childhood home and sat on the roof. She remembered seeing the plane fly above her head all those years before and her ardent wish to leave. Now she could leave, it felt different to how she imagined all those years ago.

Do you hear them passing over your head? Be careful what you wish for, Khadija. But you know what you should do, don't you? What you've always wanted. Leave here, Khadija, and never come back.

Chapter 11

A S SHE WAS PLANNING to leave, everything felt different. She ran around the streets on her morning jogs, feeling her heart and muscles get stronger. She ran and ran, seeing the streets around her change, becoming fonder of them, feeling them shrink beneath her feet. She felt guilty for thinking of how many times she had wanted to leave them behind. But now she was on her way out she wanted to remember them just as they were. She revisited her old home where she used to live and wandered around inside its empty shell. It didn't feel like the same house she lived in when she was younger. It felt smaller. It felt cold in its emptiness. She pressed her eyes shut and prayed that she would not forget what her mother looked like. How she loved her and she hadn't felt that feeling of love since she had passed. She would be separated from everything she had ever known or experienced. She glanced up to the hill-tops and considered going up to the very tops of them and confronting what lay beyond them, but she wasn't ready yet. If she had been given an opportunity for a life where she could be somebody, she wanted to take it.

The last thing on her list was saying goodbye to Saladin. She walked to the mosque and found him sitting outside, alone.

'I am leaving tomorrow.'

'Yes, I heard,' he said, standing up and dusting the earth off his trousers where he had been sat. 'I hope it is everything you want.'

Khadija didn't know what else to say and knew if she dared open her mouth to speak, it would end in tears as the lump in her throat grew. So, despite everything she had planned to say she ended up turning and walking away, leaving him still staring at the ground beneath his feet.

As Khadija was flying away from Palestine, she imagined the students receiving their grades. She always imagined that she would be there opening the envelope with them, reading out her results to herself. But she would miss that upcoming day. She would already be thousands of miles away by then. She would like to have thought she got the high ninety per cent grade that allowed her to have entry to school as a doctor. She wasn't sure how she was already on the way but her uncle had explained that Mr Masood had taken care of sending her results ahead of her to the college in Doha.

Khadija's plane landed in Doha. As she walked down the steps, she altered her mindset to feel eager to begin her new life. She tried not to even let the intense August heat make her doubt this opportunity. She was literally following in the footsteps of Iqbal Al Assad. She was going to be a student at a medical school in Doha. The airport was easy to navigate, she passed through immigration easily with her student visa and the signs all led her outside to a long queue of taxis, winding through the airport car parks. She waited in line and sat in the back of the car, the cool air streamed out of the dusty air conditioning fans and smelt of cheap seat cleaner and tobacco smoke.

'Al-Rayyan area, I have the name of the building here,' Khadija said and handed over a piece of paper with the name and street of her accommodation on it. She didn't know what to expect but the taxi driver glanced at it and began to drive. She watched out of the window as Doha passed her by in a vision of towering shiny skyscrapers that clustered around each other in different neighbourhoods of the city. Construction work, cement barriers, drilling and cranes broke up the streets and roads providing a constant backdrop of noise and dust. Typically American-style four by fours wrestled for room on the roads and mounted the curbs to get ahead of the traffic with their windows blacked out and engines roaring from their sheer size. Khadija hadn't seen so many new large cars like this before. In Palestine, cars were hard to get and those they could get their hands on were usually older with smaller engines; cheaper to run as petrol, parts and maintenance were expensive.

After twenty or thirty minutes of stop-start traffic, the taxi wound through Al-Rayyan, the area of Qatar famous for its Education City housing the newest, leading universities. However, they drove past its centre to the streets surrounding it. Apartments with old concrete balconies positioned above shops had air conditioning units attached to their walls and garments drying in the heat. They turned down a quiet residential street where apartments were replaced with villas. Palm trees and tough green shrubbery grew from the sand-coloured stone on the arid ground. The villas didn't look higher than two storeys for the most part but all Khadija could see were the villa gates, the neatly manicured gardens that had been procured outside, water pipes feeding vegetation that grew because the landscape was dry. It was so different to the land in Palestine. Here in the desert, plant life grew in wild patches of thorny harsh bushes and spiky plants that forced their way up between buildings and grit where the streets had no pavements. Shrubbery and stones gathered to the side of the roads and patches of unattended to earth filled with rubble. Every couple of streets there were mosques with small manicured courtyards, gated in and with charity bins outside. They formed part of the landscape of the neighbourhoods. The taxi dropped her off outside a low-rise villa. She walked inside the main entrance and saw it had been split off into apartments. An old sofa suite was positioned in the middle around a chipped, faux wood table in a faded cherry red. She counted six flats on the first floor and looked up to see more above. She walked over to number four and opened the door. Inside, she could see her whole space. It had a used sofa with tatty arms on one side of the wall. Just to the left of the sofa was a row of six metal cabinets, three at the top, three at the bottom with a small sink. Adjacent to that was the bathroom. She was too busy looking around to notice she had left the front door open. She panicked and ran to slam it shut. Then she leaned on the door, noticing how her pulse raced. It took a moment for the realisation to sink in that she wasn't in Palestine anymore. There was no occupation on the hilltops of Doha. There were no torchlights spinning around the hilltops at night. Just the bustle of a normal city.

In those moments when she imagined life outside of her four walls, she had the same feeling she had experienced before. Home was a temporary space. It didn't belong to her. It was a

shell where she lived for the time being. Others had lived before her and others would live there long after she was gone. It
was a strange feeling of disconnection from the world around
her. If she hadn't been so exhausted, she might have dwelt on
it longer. As it was, she fell asleep fully clothed on the sofa,
dreaming of traffic and desert.

In the morning, Khadija woke to the sounds of the call to
prayer outside the window. It startled her because she hadn't
heard it so close and loud before. She went to the window
and could see the mosque's minaret just behind the apartment
compound. She prayed *fajr* and couldn't fall back to sleep so
she went outside and took an early walk to discover her surroundings. Outside there was a narrow garden planted with a
few unloved date palms and cacti. Children had drawn chalk
drawings on the stonework that had all but faded. It looked
like they were done a while ago but the rain was not a fre-
quent visitor so the sun had bleached them out instead. A path
led from the garden and took her around to the back of the
apartment complex. Identical villas were positioned along a
man-made road that led around in a square. At the back of
the building was a basketball hoop and a small children's playground with a see-saw and swings attached. They were once
bright red but now looked a pale orange, dyed from the sun. As
the sun rose, so did the heat. The skies were a cloudless bright
blue and the heat made the atmosphere above the pavements
ripple like a mirage. Khadija walked around the compound,
ending up on the other side of her entrance having completed
the tour of the relatively small complex. She didn't see anyone
else and all their windows were mirrored so sunlight or eyes
didn't penetrate through. She walked up to the gate where a

security outpost was positioned, but no one was inside it. She peered out to the streets outside.

There were no street names, no obvious signs of where she was and she was unsure if she would find her way back if she ventured out. She walked out onto the street trying to make sure that she remembered every turn. She found nothing along the way except similar compounds and houses and still streets except for the rumble of a car that passed her infrequently. She kept walking. No one else was out on the streets to ask which direction was home. Where was she? She turned a few familiar looking corners but to no avail. She realised she hadn't brought water with her and as the heat pounded down on her head, she began to panic. No one was on the streets because it quickly became too hot during the August heat. It could reach fifty degrees, she remembered. She tried to look for shade and eventually under a broken palm tree, took cover whilst she tried to get her bearings. It all looked the same. The streets had become a maze.

A car drove past. Moments later, it drove past her again, the same car. This time it slowed down. Khadija didn't know what to do. What was about to happen?

The black window rolled down. A lady in a black *abaya* with a black chiffon headscarf spoke to her in Arabic but her accent was unfamiliar.

'Are you ok?'

Khadija didn't know what to say. She was too shy to say no but she didn't know how to get home.

'I am lost. I went for a walk but I only arrived yesterday.'

The lady climbed down from her brand-new white Nissan Patrol and beckoned for Khadija to get inside the back. She drove off with Khadija inside, stopping outside a small grocery shop and beeping outside.

After a few minutes, she handed Khadija some cold juice and a bottle of water.

'Better?'

Khadija nodded.

'I am Khalood.'

'Khadija.'

'Khadija, I love that name,' she smiled. 'Where are you staying, dear?'

Khadija told her the name of the apartment complex but she didn't know where it was.

'There is a mosque near it. It has a striped blue dome.'

Khalood now knew where it was and drove her back there.

'It is too hot here in these months, Khadija. Only go out after dusk, before *fajr*, or wait until the winter when it is cooler.'

'Thank you so much, I don't know what I would have done…'

'*Alhamdulilah*, all good is from Allah.'

Khadija climbed out and turned around to see Khalood's car still waiting until she got inside. She gave her one last wave and went inside, collapsing on the sofa and she didn't wake up for a few hours. When she did, she realised she was hungry and hadn't got any food in at all. Had she even eaten anything except for the airport pastry and fruit she had taken from the plane? She searched through her rucksack and found a packet of nuts and some dried fruit.

She needed to stock up, but this time she would get to the main road and call a taxi. As the taxi driver drove, she took note of the roads she needed to walk down to get to the busy road that ran from her neighbourhood to central Doha.

After a few weeks of settling in, Khadija had found the local supermarkets and stocked up on some basics. She had ventured out a few times since the day she was taken home and began to find a routine of making a way to the main road and turning around. She could call taxis from the main road and most of the ones around that area knew where she lived if she directed them to the mosque instead.

On her first day of term, Khadija arranged for a taxi to come and collect her an hour earlier than she was supposed to arrive. There was a bus route that could take her so it would be cheaper once she was used to the journey but for her first day, she wanted a morning that wasn't rushed or any more nerve-wracking than it had to be. Before the taxi arrived, Khadija dressed in her smartest outfit of a newish pair of trousers she had brought from the *souk* in Palestine and a blouse in off-white so she felt smart and ready. She packed her rucksack with the learning materials she had brought from Hakim's stationery shop and briefly reminded herself of her fruit bartering back home. She smiled, thinking of the amazement that her first few days of school would have led to this. She wondered what her mother would be thinking now. She knew she would be proud but not unduly; after all, there were many ways to win her mother but educational achievements paled in comparison to those of the soul. It was a brief but stinging reminder that in all her excitement she had missed her morning prayer. Khadija had no idea she would be in this position and this vigour of life accompanied her all the way to school in a surreal way, as the real streets passed by and she was being taken to the place she had always dreamt of.

Khadija saw the university campus as the taxi pulled in. She paid and climbed out, taking in the view of the modern, newly built architectural feat that sprawled out in front of her. Rectangular stone columns made a pathway to walk underneath to the university's grand entrance. In front of the imposing columns stood a sunken square fountain in the same geometrical pattern, reflecting Qatar's wealth and its Islamic history. Inside, the university opened to a huge atrium filled with light. Arabic calligraphy was inscribed on the walls, reminding those who passed through of its place in the world as an institution for creating leaders. Khadija couldn't quite believe that this was her school. She was used to a rundown classroom, with brilliant teachers, but the facilities did not look anything like these and now she was walking its halls as a student. The feeling made her stomach buzz with an extreme excitement that settled into nausea.

Students began to arrive and fill out their forms at the reception desk with plenty of helpful staff milling around in uniform with name badges on. Khadija felt nervous when the students arrived. Their clothes were either traditional Qatari dress, white robes for the men and black *abaya*s for the women, with a scent of expensive *oud* perfume worn by both, or international students in trendy bright white trainers and branded sportswear. But her fears were unfounded. She was listed, her fees were paid by a Qatari scholarship fund and she was given her campus map and classrooms.

Her class was made up of mostly locals and a few international students like her. They definitely had money, she thought.

She could tell by the huge Jeeps they climbed into outside of the school and their beautifully adorned *abaya*s that were clearly hand-embroidered. Khadija could tell by the workmanship and if that hadn't given it away, then the individually made gold signature clasps that were pinned to the back of them of the particular designer definitely did. She wondered if she were better at sewing whether she could make them; they would obviously sell for a lot. But then she remembered her cross-stitch designs and how her mother was never rich despite her fingers working and reworking the stitches day and night just to feed them. Dr Reem called her name to answer a question which snapped her back to the lecture; she briefly answered but it wasn't correct. She realised she had spent way too long looking at their clothes and how they were made. She tried to refocus and spent the rest of the lesson focusing on the projections at the front of the class and the voice of her lecturers.

The days followed the same pattern. She would get the bus in the mornings, relieved it was early enough to miss the hottest part of the day. The air conditioning on the bus barely cooled it down with the doors constantly opening and the untinted windows. She arrived at class and sat down in a row of empty seats and listened to the lecturer, making notes as she went. She noticed that some of the students had formed friendship groups and sat together in clusters. Sometimes they invited her out of politeness she thought, but Khadija preferred to be alone. She turned them down until they stopped asking, preferring to go and sit in the library. In the afternoon heat, she would take the bus home and arrive at her empty apartment where she still lived out of her suitcase. She made simple dinners she had cooked from childhood, of rice or lentils and soups she had made her ailing mother. She realised she hadn't learnt the recipes she loved the most and had no idea how to cook them. She wished she had paid more attention to her mama when she was in the kitchen creating her favourites. It made her homesick to imagine the food of home and the delicious waft of freshly fried falafel and the taste of pickled cabbage inside freshly baked bread. The thought made her stomach grumble. And at home, the fruit was juicy and bursting with flavour. Here it was dry and already browning the moment it was cut open.

Chapter 12

WEEKS PASSED AND HER routine remained unchanged. Surrounded by books in the library, she tried to take her mind off home. Instead, she researched anatomy, looked into the science behind the workings of organs to discover what she didn't understand. The body, a miracle machine, placed together, its heart beating at its centre. But despite her best intentions, her mind would wander. It would wander back to the bird's heart. Then it would escape the walls of the houses and wander back to the rolling fields of home where the hills and gradient land would rise and fall and she would know each of its crevices and dips. She would know each time the fruit was ready to be harvested, she could feel the red soil under her toes. Sometimes she would be back on her rooftop or sneaking out when her mother was there. She missed the voice of the storyteller and the history of her land. She missed knowing that Jerusalem shared the same land space as them, where all her stories of hope had originated from. She thought of Amina. Of where she was now and what she would be doing. Still, her future was bound to change from the freedom of childhood and now it was full of possibilities she could never imagine, in a city full of its own riches and she couldn't let them slip through her fingers. And with that positive thought reverberating through her mind, she left and instead of going straight home, she decided to stop by the mall and grab something to eat. She wouldn't usually be so frivolous with her money; Doha wasn't a cheap city to live in, but she felt she had earned it. Maybe she would find some falafel? Or something hot and inviting that reminded her of home.

She grabbed a taxi and it took her to the main mall in the city, the Villagio. She had heard the name before but didn't expect to find a piece of Venice built in the middle of the Arabian Gulf. She read the information poster on how the mall was styled on the streets of the Italian town built on the water. She stared at the images on the poster of old brick houses with water lapping up to their doorways. She looked at the photographs of the town, all connected with a series of bridges and the rivers that ran through them, carrying people on narrow boats. Inside she was hit by the icy cold air conditioning that cooled her to her core as she walked around, her shoes clicking against the marble effect floor that wound through the waterways of Venice. The shop windows displayed expensive luxury items she had only seen as copies in the *souk*s back home. Dior, Chanel and Gucci shops showcased leather bags and designer coats and jewels. The prices weren't on them and Khadija did not dare even go inside the shops because she knew that they would take one look at her and know she couldn't afford such things. She wondered who could. Who could spend thousands of pounds on a handbag when there were people back home who couldn't afford to eat?

In the middle, the wide aisles were broken up with elaborate fountains. Khadija leaned over a bridge joining one walkway to another and watched as a blue river canal wound through the length of the mall. She watched as couples and families sat in gondolas being rowed through the mock Venetian streets. She glanced upwards to a romantically painted sky framed in the archways of the ceiling. What a world they had made here. One where it felt as if you had stepped inside another city. She felt as if she had finally escaped. She had left behind the dark hillside, travelled to another country and found herself on the streets of an Arabian Venice.

It was during those musing moments of trailing the mall and sitting on the gondolas as they were rowed through the water that she thought of her mother. Why had she not sought out more of a life? She could never ask her now why she chose to stay behind and have a child. Why had she not chosen to travel and see the world and everything it had to offer? Why would anyone choose to stay behind?

Her days had become like a mirage. She no longer went home to the dingy walls of the apartment, instead preferring to escape to the shops and streets of the mock Venetian walkways where she could eat something hot and prepared quickly, developing a taste for the convenience it offered when she was too exhausted or bored to cook for herself. As she ate, she watched life pass as she saw families with multiple children around their feet in matching clothes. She saw couples hand-in-hand, meandering through the walkways with drinks in their spare hands, or spending time sitting outside on the courtyards that were roped off to mimic outdoor streets complete with lanterns and outdoor plants and trees. She imagined what it would be like not to be alone.

At university, she was falling behind in her studies. No matter how much time she invested in trying to read, it was like her mind was blank and information just wouldn't sink in. Her mind drifted. She thought back to her uncle's words. 'You're nothing but a daydreamer.'

It wasn't meant in a nice way. But it was true. She had trouble focusing. Her mind would drift off back to the old stories she was told as a child. Her mind would be in the present, listening to the lecturer then it would snap back to her home, inside her tiny mother's house where she would be making her tea. She would refocus. She would remind herself how her goal was in reach but the thought of the years ahead of study exhausted her. Then it went to the hilltops. To a spool of blue thread. After the calmness that followed when she changed country, the nightmares had returned. She thought of the graveyard, of the torch beams swimming around the night sky, getting closer and closer.

She spent more time in the mall. She would close her eyes at night and imagine she was on the canals of Venice. She would escape across the Arabian Sea and be so far away physically, but the lights would follow her wherever she went.

Some days at the mall she would wander past the expensive *abaya* shops. There were women back home wearing them, but here in Doha, they were made of a beautiful wash of silken black. She longed to look at her plain self in the same way. To be draped in black satin, a veil of anonymity so she could be whoever she wanted to be. Everyone who knew who she really was, weren't there to see her reinvention. She could experiment. She wandered through the door where the smell of *oud* floated around the dresses. She pulled back the rack, one after another, looking at the delicate embroidery, the black lace laid

115

upon black silk, the beads and crystals stitched up throughout the backs of the dresses, the matching chiffon headscarf.

'Can I help you?' a shop assistant came over asking, and Khadija instantly felt embarrassed. She couldn't afford one and everyone would know that. They would know that she wasn't beautiful or special, just a village girl whose name no one would remember. So, it was to Khadija's surprise that the assistant put them up against her and took a few to the changing area, swinging the curtain to the side and hanging them inside. Khadija stepped inside. The curtain was closed and Khadija was left looking at herself in the mirrors. She slipped off her jacket and put an *abaya* on and wrapped it over her body like a cloak. She tucked her hair behind her ears and secured it in a knot below her neck and wrapped the black scarf around her face. She looked at herself in the mirror. She saw a young woman who was yet to know who she would become. She had shaken off some of her past, she could reinvent herself into someone new. Then she looked at the price tag. She took it off and put it back on the hanger, leaving so quickly she almost ran out of the store. The taxi dropped her off on the main road. As she walked towards her apartment, the loud engines of the cars roared past her, the lights and beeps in chaos all around. She felt foolish to think she was anyone different.

It didn't take too long to become frustrated in the well-lit malls that glittered with temptation that she could never afford. She didn't have extra money to shop and she had walked it so many times, she knew it inside out. She could hear her footsteps echoing on the cold floor. Her feet always in a pair of shoes. Never free to roam. She realised she needed to be outside more to reconnect with herself. She swapped her shoes for the battered running trainers she had brought and instantly smiled, not realising how the little part of home she brought lifted her spirits.

She spent the following winter evenings jogging through the streets. The weather had cooled and it had become a perfect time to get outside and explore without the fear of it becoming too unbearably hot. Her old habits of managing her pulse rate returned automatically. She was less fit; she had to give up the convenience food and begin taking care of her health once more. She didn't want a weak heart. She jogged and as she did, she saw the real Doha. She cut down side lanes and through the Arab neighbourhoods of villa compounds and houses guarded by huge towering gates, adorned with lights all around them. She jogged past petrol station forecourts that were the hub of the city. They had American fast-food chains around the centre of the petrol pumps serving everything from burgers and milkshakes, doughnut shops and frozen yoghurt stalls to more local falafel or rice and meat dishes. Khadija didn't want to eat any more fast food, she thought, resisting the waft of hot fried food that filled the forecourts. Huge off-road trucks and jeeps packed into them beeping for food deliveries or for fuel service. The lights there were constant, hurried and busy.

She had discovered her area on her evening and morning jogging trips. She had become familiar with the local villas in the Arab neighbourhoods like the one she lived amongst. She noticed that their lights switched on automatically at dusk. That in this bright, busy city, they still kept the lights on wrapping around their villas until dawn broke. She ran until she hit the coast and watched the waves crash against the rocks. She sat on the dark grey sand and smelt the unfamiliar smell of the ocean as it rolled into the shore. She stumbled upon the old *souk*, tucked away off the main road. Its winding streets filled with merchandise, small shops, expensive carpets, Qatari dress and local camel rides for the tourists. She liked it there, meandering through the streets, it took her back to what the streets of Jerusalem looked like to her. The old Middle Eastern market towns, the crowds of people, the noises and smells of food and incense. She wound down until she reached another section of the old *souk*, selling rabbits, chickens, fish, and then as she approached the end, the birds squawked and flitted between the cages. The heat increased under the stone archways that enclosed this section of the *souk*, the air felt heavy and suffocating. She turned around to see where she came from, if she could turn around and escape back to fresh air but the *souk* was packed; she couldn't leave the way she had arrived. She became disorientated. Words flew around her as it became busier, she was in the way, she had to move. She tried to run past the birds, she didn't want to see them in their cages. She heard their bodies banging against the bars, their shrill calls pierced the air. She thought of Taha's. She thought of another scene. One where caged birds squawked and bashed against cages in sheer panic. Piled on top of each other, their cages trapping them in.

The storyteller's voice was back, as clear as it was ringing through the rooftops back in Palestine:

You didn't listen to your mother, did you? You didn't hear what she had to tell you. Did you need to cut open the bird? Were you really trying to save it or is there evil in you? Remember Angel Jibrael removed a clot from Prophet Mohammed's (peace be upon him) heart. Do you remember that clot was the devil clinging to his heart? You must have evil in your heart, Khadija. Maybe that is what the secret is. Maybe that is what you are running from. You are running, aren't you? You are lost in this maze-like city and you have searched all four corners of it but you haven't found what you are looking for because it isn't here.

She stumbled into the section of the *souk* that was open to the skies. She looked up, took deep breaths but the desert air that night meant relief didn't come quickly. She centred herself and tried to take her mind off it. It wasn't real, just her childhood stories coming back to haunt her, but they couldn't reach her here. The army couldn't, the occupation couldn't, she had become lost in the streets of another country. She walked through the streets, rifling through packed stalls with binoculars, compasses, lanterns, figures and trinkets. She found another one with leather-bound books and found a copy of poems by Mahmoud Darwish. She read the price on the back, twenty Qatari riyals. She bought it and left, flicking through the pages, finding similarities between his displacement and her missing of a home she was able to get back to. The *athan* began to call out over the *souk*. One after another, only seconds apart, another *athan* sounded somewhere in the distance, then another. Khadija stopped and strained her ears to listen to all the voices ringing in the air. It was a futile hope she held on to that one of them might be his even though she knew it was a completely unlikely situation that she would hear his voice. But students of knowledge did come to Qatar to learn Islam. They could be destined to be together, couldn't they?

She began a slow walk home. Her body felt tired and she realised she had covered a lot of ground. Her street came into view. Just as she was about to turn the corner, she saw the figure of someone she recognised. A walk unquestionably unique that belonged to someone she knew. The figure wound through a street into a quieter residential area. Khadija followed. 'Mama?' She knew it couldn't be, but the streets were dark. The figure didn't turn around when she called out.

She disappeared around the side of the mosque on the streets adjacent to her apartment. She recognised its dark emerald green dome. She walked through a gated door that had a sign outside, 'Markaz Maymoona'. Khadija walked inside into a small hallway. In the centre was a table full of leaflets, books, large posters pinned up on the walls. She picked them up and read them. Quran reading classes, Arabic classes, Tajweed for Beginners, Coming to Islam. She picked up a few and leafed through them, reading the course lists. A group of sisters laughing together passed her and said *salam* as she left. A twinge of sadness reminded her she didn't really know anyone in Doha. She had lived there for months now and yet the majority of her days were spent alone. She had followed the figure here; it reminded her of her mama. She had lost touch with her mother's only comfort; her faith. It had been her hope. And here she was in Doha, wasting her time in the malls, wasting her education.

'*Salam alaikom, rahmatullahi wa barakatu*,' a voice said.

She turned around to see the woman she had followed.

'*Wa alaikom salam.* I'm sorry, I shouldn't be here. I thought you were… someone else.'

'That's ok, dear. Which one are you interested in?'

'Oh, I can't afford any courses. I'm training to be a doctor.'

There wasn't even a flinch on her face of being impressed. That was usually the standard response Khadija had quite enjoyed eliciting as though she had something, no, everything, to prove.

'These courses are paid for, dear. You don't need to pay. Are you usually free this time on Thursday evenings?'

Khadija was ashamed to lie. She heard her mother's voice, *the angels step away from you if you lie,* so she agreed.

'Well, why don't you sign up for my class? It starts next week.'

She handed Khadija a leaflet. She said yes and followed her instructions to fill out the form. Khadija felt as if she couldn't say no. As if saying no would disappoint her just as she disappointed everyone else. When Khadija thought about it, passing the mosque on the way home, she realised that she was as disappointed in herself.

She took the leaflet home with her and read the front. The Arabic writing read, 'The heart.' Khadija couldn't help thinking of the series of events that had led to that moment; she stumbled upon the centre, following a figure she thought was her mother and now had a feeling that she would be compelled to return. Perhaps she would just sit through one class and then she would be able to discount it and move on. With her heart in so much turmoil, she would at least try. It wasn't as if her evenings were filled with much else and the company would do her good.

Chapter 13

DESPITE THE HELP FROM her teacher, Khadija was struggling with her coursework as she tried to process the information she learnt in class. Her fears were confirmed when her teacher pulled her aside to discuss her latest results. 'Khadija, I've noticed you have been struggling. Your grades haven't been consistent with your predicted ones. Is there anything you want to talk about?'

Dr Reem was probably the exact type of person Khadija would talk to if there was anything wrong but she didn't because she didn't know what to say. She thought of her uncle and wondered what exactly he had agreed to with Mr Masood that enabled her to have a scholarship to be rid of her. Dr Reem interrupted her thoughts. 'Has anything happened back home?'

She remembered Saladin. She hadn't heard anything from home in so long. She hadn't expected to since there weren't really many people left there that would be interested in her day-to-day life. Perhaps they would if she went back and she was someone as important as a doctor.

'I don't think so. But I haven't been sleeping well.'

'Why do you think that is?'

'I see the lights when I close my eyes. It keeps me awake.'

Dr Reem pursed her lips together as if she was trying to imagine what Khadija was saying.

'Sometimes children of trauma—'

'Oh, I'm not a child of a trauma.'

Dr Reem looked taken aback and leaned back in her chair, grabbing a file from her desk, flicking through the pages of it. She re-read it with her eyebrows furrowed as if desperately trying to work something out.

'I am sure it is just a new place away from home.'

'Ok, but if you do think it will help, we have a counsellor who is trained to—'

'I'm sure it's just the place.'

'Well, it can be quite loud at night. Try to close your blinds, close out the light. But you can talk to me.'

'I appreciate it. Thank you.'

Khadija smiled at her, noticing that it made Dr Reem smile a little as though in a small way she had helped.

'As you're on the scholarship scheme, you must hit a seventy-five per cent average but we will give it longer… considering your circumstances.'

Khadija considered her circumstances were her being an orphan, but she would take it. She would accept help with anything that kept her there and on her way to success.

She left the room and didn't go to the library. Her head was already pounding from the stress of potential failure that had now come to light. Her hands were clammy and her disappointment made her feel sick. If she wasn't a doctor, what was she? Who was she?

She walked along the streets near her neighbourhood, passing the Markaz Maymoona Centre. The *athan* called from the adjacent mosque. The amplified call to prayer beat through her, stirring something inside her. She took out her phone and dialled home.

'Uncle? It's Khadija?'

'Who?'

'Khadija, in Doha.'

'Have you run out of money?' her uncle asked.

'No, uncle. I have stayed in the scholarship budget. It is plenty for–'

'Have they got rid of you?' he interrupted, through spluttered coughs.

Khadija waited for him to finish.

'No, I just wanted to call to hear a voice from home. How is everyone there? Have you heard from Amina… or maybe Saladin?' Khadija winced, realising how obvious it sounded but she couldn't take her words back now.

He paused. He completely ignored the enquiry about Amina. He had a tendency to pretend that people he didn't like, didn't exist.

'Saladin, the Sheikh's son?'

'Yes.' Khadija's voice shook a little.

'Yes, yes,' he said with unusual vigour, 'I hear he is engaged.'

Khadija fell silent.

After another brief coughing spell, he continued, 'To that good-looking girl. She was in your class, the girl whose parents have that expensive house, that big, sprawling thing a few streets away.'

'Aliya?'

'I don't know her name, but I think that's the one. Yes, you hear things around the village. Everyone is always in each other's business here.' He muttered the last few words. Khadija couldn't make them out. He often continued talking to himself without registering he was part of a conversation.

'Yes, they are.' Khadija's voice was barely a whisper. She felt sick.

'Is that it?'

'My grades, did you receive them at home?'

'So, you are a failure?'

'I just wanted to know what they were.'

'I don't know. I had nothing to do with it. Just be grateful you have this opportunity and don't mess it up.'

And with that, he hung up the phone. Khadija held the phone to her ear, listening to the silence. She turned around and wandered around the streets, trying to process the information. It was already dark, but the lights from the cars and the heavy thrum of traffic meant there was no solace to be found in it. She wondered why Saladin would marry Aliya? They didn't even like each other. It made sense though. Her family had money. He was there. She was there. She imagined the wedding would be in the summer. She imagined the fields being set up with a huge marquee, the streets closed from all the guests' cars blocking it, the frantic wedding plans and henna parties and the crowds of people celebrating and wishing them well. She hadn't ever considered marriage but it only compounded her loneliness and isolation now. She wondered how she would feel being a bride. Being the most beautifully dressed in the room. Having the villagers notice her and congratulating her on becoming a woman. Becoming someone in the community. She hadn't really seen a wedding in her future. She had been so set on leaving. She was so convinced that the place itself was the root cause of her heartache and the vacuous feeling that seemed to haunt her. She thought she might find herself in a long-lasting career, in the prestigious title, in the power it had to help others but she felt as powerless as ever. All her university class was teaching her was that sometimes patients lived and sometimes they died. She thought she would wield an almost supernatural strength to tackle life. It hadn't happened yet.

She checked the time. If she hurried, she wouldn't be too late to make the class at the Markaz Centre. She rushed back through the streets, following the minaret of the green mosque that she remembered positioned in front of it. She walked in, out of breath, and searched the classroom doors until she saw number five. The classroom it was held in. She opened the door, hoping to sneak inside unnoticed but as soon as she did, the sister stopped talking and they all looked at her. It was at these moments that Khadija wished her invisibility skills were back from childhood. They were all facing her and then a sister pushed out her chair and came over, shaking her hand and welcoming her to an empty desk. Her gloved hands were soft and her voice spoke in English with an accent. She was ushered to sit down amidst a flurry of welcomes and handshakes and sat in the welcoming glow of the classroom light, surrounded by women, relieved she was no longer outside roaming the streets.

For the next few months of school, Khadija was more determined than ever. There was still hope. She could read the books again. She could spend her evenings studying, watching videos and lectures. She could make it. It wasn't over. In fact, the thought of seeing Aliya and telling her the news, 'Doctor Khadija', was enough. She walked back home every day and spent the nights reading her notes and poring over the pages of her books.

She was present in class. She was focused. There was nothing that was going to break her dreams. Certainly not Aliya. Her grades were picking up. She slept at night through sheer exhaustion. When the lights began to swim around her head, forcing her to wake up in panic and sweat, she wouldn't dwell on it. She would switch on the light and work through it. Whatever it was in her past that was trying to surface, was not going to threaten her future.

As the months passed fresh air never seemed to alleviate the thickness of the desert heat, exacerbated by the constant rumble of cars and electricity whirring from the air conditioning units attached to every apartment, every villa, every building. It created a soundtrack to the city, a twenty-four-hour relentless beat of noise and heat.

When the evenings came for her weekly class at the Markaz Maymoona, she was one of the first to arrive inside to the warm lights glowing from the classroom. The class timings changed with the prayer times, so when Khadija learnt that they would pray in the green dome mosque beforehand, she began to meet them there and prayed with them before class.

The classes were taught with gentleness, slowly and considered to adapt for the language barriers with the international class of mixed women. Throughout the evenings they began to get to know each other more. Khadija introduced herself. 'A trainee doctor from Palestine, on a scholarship in Doha.'

She beamed inside with pride. She wasn't sure why because it didn't seem to fit her yet, but it sounded respectful. Something to be in awe of. The sister sitting next to her went next. 'I am a mother of five. It used to be six, but I lost one last year.' She began to cry and it was followed suit by others as she gave them details of what had happened. The teacher stepped forward. 'She will pull you to paradise.'

Khadija felt a hole begin to tear in her heart.

During the evenings, it cooled enough for her to go out. She visited the old *souk* and strolled around becoming lost in the stalls and the merchandise, the restaurants and the throng of people walking outside in the cooler evening air. She found an authentic Italian restaurant tucked away under one of the alcoves and sat outside its courtyard eating Italian pasta. She savoured the sweet roasted tomatoes and the rich cheeses inside the soft pasta casings and barely remembered those times she went hungry as a child. She sat on a table for one under a hanging tree, watching as people walked by and dined together. She wondered if this was what it felt like to grow and experience life. She would never have done this a few years ago and now, here she was, sitting in a rustic Italian-style restaurant eating food she hadn't tasted before. She wondered if her old school friends could see her now. They might even be envious of her; an international student, free and living in a new country. No one would have guessed the girl they pushed into the grave would leave them all behind, just as she told them she would. Things were beginning to fall into a rhythm of comfort.

Ramadan and Eid followed with the sisters from the Markaz Centre surprising her after classes at the weekend with trays of homemade food. Her tiny apartment had never had so much food inside it. She packaged up what she couldn't eat and gave it to the labourers that often passed by the compound, waiting for their transport home after a gruelling day's work.

There was an ache inside her though that missed how captivating home was during those blessed days. She missed the open sky, free of noise and traffic. She missed the rolling fields where she was the only person on them for miles around. She missed all of its wonder. She wondered if she would ever feel the same about home like she did when she was a child.

Her trip home was almost upon her so that helped because she would have the opportunity to feel its ground underneath her feet again. Khadija spent most of her final weeks before the holidays selecting a carefully picked outfit in the mall. She wanted everyone to know that she had become someone. She wanted to look different to the girl that they were used to. Gone were her ill-fitting shoes, replaced with new ones, soft leather. Expensive looking. She was returning not as orphan Khadija, but as someone who had escaped her shadow self and become a young, confident woman. She could fake the confident bit. I mean, who would really know? It was a two-week trip back and she had decided she would go and find out where Amina was. She missed her. She also thought that maybe Amina could fill in the gaps of missing information she had about her uncle and her mother's old house. She packed her bags and closed up her apartment for the break. She had a brief moment to consider the contrast. Doha was safe so it wasn't a concern of hers to leave what little she had behind. It wasn't usual for empty houses to become occupied in other countries.

Chapter 14

THE FLIGHT TO AMMAN, Jordan went as scheduled. But because the flight only got her to Amman, from there she would have to cross into Palestine. It was one of the few border crossings where Palestinians were allowed to enter. Tel Aviv airport was not an option unless you wanted to face hours of delays and even more invasive checks when you landed. Most Palestinians she knew would avoid the airport so it was natural that this would be her intended route. Upon arrival, she took a taxi that would drive through the city towards the border. Passing through the city, the low lying farms, the hills and rocky unlevelled land, the landscape, reminded her at once of home, when this part of the world stretched with no borders and it was easy to imagine it as part of one land. It was so geographically similar to Jericho she imagined the Bedouin wandering this far.

She passed by the open-fronted shops, sparks flying from soldered metal, grimy car parts being sold second-hand and supermarkets selling beach ware to tourists where brightly coloured inflatables of flamingos and palm trees seemed to stand out on the sun-battered stalls. As she passed it all, she looked at her reflection in the window; she didn't look that different to the girl who had left.

They pulled up at the bridge and she stepped out. A young woman came to her, wrapped in shawls with a baby in her arms. Khadija turned around to see the taxi driver had lifted her suitcase out and was already driving away. She watched him disappear down the road.

'Money to feed us, for the baby. Feed us, God reward you.'

She shuffled around in her pockets before pulling out coins and dropping them in her hands.

'Dirham, dirhams?'

Khadija noticed the coins were riyals from Doha. 'I'm sorry that's all I have.'

The woman started shouting at her in a language she didn't understand. The commotion attracted a guard from the bridge. Two of them stood side by side with rifles swinging on their shoulders. Their boots kicked the sand, whilst they puffed smoke from cigarettes hanging from the corner of their lips. Khadija saw them watching her through creased brows. They looked her up and down and the woman next to her. They pressed their hands against their rifles and spoke to each other before walking towards her.

She was alone at the border. She glanced behind her at the car rental shops, the road going only one way, back to Amman or ahead to Palestine. At the border, she knew what the bridge crossing was like. Rows of Israeli soldiers, watchtowers, rows of barbed wire, impenetrable security. If they didn't let you pass through, you didn't pass through. For those few minutes she stood, she saw her life span in two directions. One where she made it home. The other, like countless before her, left stranded. This small strip of securitised land separated them from their homes and families. If she couldn't get through, what would she do? What had others done? Tried to pass and then been imprisoned? Or stayed in Jordan? Tried to make a living and build a life but every time they glanced at the horizon they could see the glimmers of home like a mirage in the distance. A mirage that showed them their ancestral homes. Their orchards and olive trees. The loved ones left behind, both dead and alive. And all they could do was watch from afar, only to realise that the glimmers in the distance were the drops of white phosphorus raining down.

Khadija grabbed her suitcase handle, her hands now clammy under the strap. She walked nervously, out of sync, as though her footsteps were exposing her. As though just for claiming to be Palestinian she was a fraud. A fake. Someone who didn't deserve to exist.

She dragged her suitcase through and unfolded the pages of her passport. 'I'm going to my hometown, outside Ramallah,' she said, as she stopped at the guards. The security guards looked at her and waved her past. She walked down towards the passport control booths. She saw a group of backpackers in linen slacks, what looked like a religious entourage, heading to Jerusalem, she thought. She walked on. Tourists were spared the excessive checks, although it wasn't uncommon for it to take hours for them to pass through in busy periods during the summer. But Palestinians had their own lines, their own buses. They took triple the time to pass through security and checks. The heat intensified as she waited for her passport to be stamped for the Palestinian-only bus. This part didn't bother her too much. It was the next section she didn't like, the part where they crossed into Israeli hands, where it all changed. The young army soldiers in matching new uniforms. Bigger guns.

More security. More interview cells to be questioned in. More border arrests. She stood outside the glass as the Israeli guard called someone else to have a look at her passport. She was told to wait.

She sat behind families, lone travellers. They sat unaffected. The kids laughed and ate sweets as their mother read a magazine and fanned herself with the pages as she bounced a baby on her lap. A journalist was on the phone complaining loudly about her treatment which seemed to fall on deaf ears. They waited. She waited. She watched the hall. Some people were let through but mostly they were held or sent to the waiting rooms. She remembered the storyteller's voice, '*They do it to arrest doctors and engineers, scientists and surgeons. They don't want them coming back to Palestine and building it up even stronger.*'

She watched as they pulled one young man to the side. He was in a T-shirt proudly displaying the Palestinian flag. 'Get your hands off me,' he shouted. They held his arm tighter. Two more guards came. He disappeared into a room to the side of the booths. He shouted his name out, 'Mohammed Rasheed. Ramallah. Tell my family if I don't make it out.'

Khadija looked around to see who he was talking to, but she couldn't see anyone. She repeated it to herself. Mohammed. Rasheed. Ramallah. Mohammed. Rasheed. Ramallah. The name echoed around her head. She could be the only one who had heard it. She mustn't forget. Mohammed. Rasheed. Ramallah.

She remembered Ramallah. She remembered visiting the Darwish museum. She remembered some of the writing on the walls. '*Absence teaches me its lesson.*' Her memory had returned to Palestine, to Doha, and back to the metal chair of the waiting room. Her thoughts were interrupted by a soldier who led her back to the passport booth.

Her passport was stamped 'Palestinian Authority Areas only' which meant she was only allowed in the West Bank and not allowed to enter Jerusalem. She made it through to the suitcase hall and watched as her case was lifted and placed aside, away from the carousel. She checked the label and dragged it outside, relieved to be out of the building and able to see the light blue of the sky above her head. The blacked-out buses were waiting in the lines outside with their routes written on cards and laid inside their front window screens. The heat from the exhaust and the fumes hung thick in the air, turning the trails into a smoky ripple. She checked the number for her village as the driver tossed her bag underneath the bus. She sat staring at her reflection in the window. Would anyone notice if she disappeared? How long would it take them? Would they just assume she hadn't returned from Doha as promised? Saladin might have noticed if it was back in their school days. But probably not now. Suddenly, the intense sun reminded her. Summer was wedding season. If they had been engaged as her uncle said, then maybe it was going to happen whilst she was there? She began to feel uncomfortable in her seat. She looked out of the window, back to the passport office. Could she get back through from here? It was always easier leaving Palestine than trying to get in.

She stood up, but other passengers climbed onto the bus, finding their seats and forcing her back to hers as they tried to squeeze through the coach aisle. When they had found their seats and stowed their bags, she tried again but it was busier. She darted off, taking the slim chance that she had and went to a guard standing outside the building. 'Excuse me.' Her meek voice even irritated her. She never seemed to get anyone's attention. 'I need to get back,' she shouted, almost aimlessly as the guard just shook his head, pointed towards the buses and walked inside. The automatic doors closed behind him and left her to stand in the outdoor heat as her new top and jacket clung to her body, sticking to her sweat underneath them. She jogged back to the bus. Her case was on there and it was pulling off. She hammered on the doors and found an empty seat. As she did, her mind spun with images. She imagined the two of them standing in front of his father, the Imam. Saladin smiling at his new bride. Aliya turning to look at her. Her beautiful face, smiling to the room, but it would seek her out and her smile would curl ever so slightly so she could prove that she had won their unspoken rivalry once and for all. She couldn't go. She couldn't watch. She wondered how her uncle would be now. She thought maybe he was proud. Maybe he wanted to show her off. His once disobedient niece, the wild daydreamer; look at her now, a trainee doctor. But her mind altered when she remembered she lived like a ghost in his house. She thought of the day when she proposed to Saladin. What shame and embarrassment that must have put upon him to have a girl so bold as to ask a boy that. A girl with nothing to give, except herself. Did everyone know about that too? Her cheeks flushed violently so she pressed them against the window to try and cool them down. Outside, she noticed the bus had stopped again. They were still in Jordan. They hadn't crossed over.

'Wait, wait!' she shouted, running over to the bus driver whilst banging the exit door. She was out of breath so she couldn't get her words out.

'You need to sit down.'

'I need to get my bags off.'

'You will have to sit down. They are watching,' the driver said, as he gestured to the security around them. The concrete walls topped with barbed wire, the watch towers, the guns. Stumbling back to her seat, she tried to catch her breath. The other passengers were unusually silent as the bus drove through a military gate and entered the other side. She sat down and tried to catch her breath but as the bus bumped along, all she could see was the armed guards in the turrets. The reflective glare of the huge lights that rotated around them, spinning, spinning. Even though it was bright daylight, the reflections still shone and all the movement made her sick into her bag.

The bus pulled up outside of her old village. She didn't want to go to her uncle's house so she walked to the only other place she knew. Her old house that she shared with her mother. It had been left for so long now that if she hadn't looked hard enough and if she didn't know its precise location as well as she did, she wouldn't have recognised it. Consumed by the overgrowth around it, nature had crept in and swallowed it. Taken from the living, it belonged to another world that humans didn't inhabit now. '*Don't leave your houses,*' the voice echoed. She went around to the back door that she had smashed open the previous summer with Saladin. She kept her sight firmly on the interior of the house. Not once did she look at the hilltop.

Inside, the hole in the wall had been hammered open even more than when she had discovered it with Saladin that day. A gust of cold air sent a shiver through her body as she tentatively stepped inside.

Behind the broken wall, the space opened to form a narrow alleyway; she was sandwiched between her windowless lounge wall and another brick wall. She walked down it. She estimated it to be the same length as the brick wall that ran around its circumference. But what was it? Why was there a narrow passageway between the old wall and her house?

She found nothing that revealed its secret. She remembered how when she was young, her summers went on the pursuit of wild stories, spies and covered truths. The reality was an encroaching occupation, a dark history and one that had become synonymous with displacement. On the floor was an Israeli tourist brochure. It showed a gleaming harbour, brand new homes and newly built swimming pools filled to the brim with water. Her feet ached on the parched ground. She threw down the brochure and climbed back into the old space she had spent so much time in. So much time staring at the walls and not seeing what lay behind them. Her mother had kept her away from the ruins. Why had she kept it from her? What did she want to tell her all those years ago?

She wandered around her old childhood home looking for anything else it could have hidden from her. She opened the bathroom door and stepped inside. The pale tiles had moss growing between the cracks. The sink stood unaffected, while the mirror above it had become mottled with the passing seasons of heat and cold. The shower had snapped off the wall under its own weight, as the grouting had broken behind it. It had fallen onto an old chair. A plastic chair that sat with a puddle of water in the middle. Khadija remembered how hard it had been to lift her mother, so eventually, she washed her from that chair. She began to cry. All her mother's work, her whole life, and then for it to end. Her tiny house, at the bottom of the hilltop. Now Khadija was there, she began to see her own life play out in front of her. Only she didn't have a child. She clasped her hands on her empty stomach. She cried for her mother and she cried for herself. For a future she couldn't yet see.

She left the bathroom and changed out of her clothes. She had a spare set; although not ideally what she wanted everyone to see her in, she actually felt better in a more subdued outfit of loose black trousers and a long-sleeved blouse that she tucked into her waistband. She grabbed a delicate chiffon *hijab* and wrapped it around her head. She had to clear her head before she arrived at her uncle's. It was a long enough walk for her to practise her composed reaction on hearing the news that Saladin was about to be married and that she would be attending the wedding. Because there, as in other parts of Palestine, a wedding was a celebrated village event. The joining together of two families, the joy of young love and young marriage. The hope it brought for future generations of children who would replace their footsteps in the houses and streets. That, in a land that was being eroded daily, was one of their collectively celebrated moments. There was no way Khadija could not attend. And if she didn't it would be obvious that it was too painful for her and she wouldn't let Aliya have the satisfaction. That summer was Khadija's. It belonged to her and she was there to show everyone just how far she had come and she wasn't going to let her win. She walked down the hill towards the street of her uncle's house. The heat had subsided and given way to a breeze smelling of cherry blossom and baked bread. She strolled past the mosque and briefly wondered if Saladin was there before the call to prayer rang out. She walked on a little slower, but it must have been some time until the next prayer so she carried on, only slightly disappointed that she hadn't seen him. It wouldn't be long, she thought. But she had to get home, as surely her uncle, despite his moods, must have been expecting her. She took a breath at the door and knocked hard on her uncle's door, with purpose.

No one answered. She tried again but this time the door just opened from the force of her knock. She walked inside the hallway and was met by its shadow once again. It closed from the outside and she was back in its ominous presence. She had dug around in its secrets and still it had revealed nothing. She shuddered. She went back outside and sat on the lawn. The view outside was less oppressive. The sun began to sink overhead and she watched as it fell down by the horizon, painting the sky in all its beautiful glory before sinking into the soil. She daydreamed of the fields and the smell of ripened cherries and the taste of the sweet juice squeezed once picked from the trees. She felt the soft grass underneath her bare feet, the sky spanning above her in bands of blue and gold.

'If it isn't Khadija, returning to her homeland,' a voice said, playfully.

Khadija opened her eyes and heard the familiar voice repeat the sentence. She looked at the face watching her from the darkness. She saw the lights of the mosque in the distance and further behind him the illuminated hillside. It must have been late.

'Saladin?'

'Yes, who else would stay behind and follow so easily in his father's footsteps?'

Khadija managed a faint laugh, embarrassed by her predicament. She had imagined many scenarios of Saladin seeing her back home. Down at the market, wearing her new outfit. Sitting in a café looking relaxed and happy. Reading under a tree in the orchard. Asleep on the front of her uncle's lawn in the middle of the night, was not one.

'Only you would be able to sleep out on the grass in the dark like the true country girl I know so well.'

She stood up quickly and brushed herself down. 'I'd better go in, I bet my uncle is looking for me.'

'Probably not. He left a few days ago.'

'What? Where did he go?'

Saladin shrugged his shoulders.

'Oh, ok. Well, I will stay here until tomorrow and work out what to do next. I'm sure he won't be long.'

'So, how is life as a high-flying international student? I didn't think we would see you again.'

'Yes, it's great,' Khadija answered, but she knew her voice fell flat. 'I mean, yes, it's really great.'

'So, are you planning on coming back when you are qualified?'

'Oh, that is a long time away.'

'It goes quickly though. I thought you would have forgotten about us already,' he said, shoving his hands in his pockets.

'I guess you've all been too busy getting on with your own lives to consider giving me a second thought.' Khadija was now adjusting her scarf and brushing down her clothes roughly. 'It's not like I ever fitted in. I was more of a black sheep. Not like you lot.'

'Wow, you *have* completely forgotten me then.'

'Why would I give you all a second thought? I am busy there, you know. I have a chance for a future too.'

'I always knew you would become someone strong. You always were fierce. Never let anything get you down. Always knew what you wanted.'

'Seems like you do too.'

'Ok…' Saladin paused, as though he had something else to say, but Khadija didn't want to hear it. She moved back a few steps so Saladin wouldn't see the hurt in her face or hear the disappointment making her heart beat so loud that she was sure he could hear it. Khadija imagined seeing Aliya's face beaming because of their engagement, making her heartbeat increase. She couldn't think. She didn't know what to say. 'So, I'm going to get back but I will see you…'

'Yes, of course. *Salam*,' Khadija said and practically jogged to the house and slammed the door behind her. She didn't dare look back. She didn't want to look at the window and see his face, despondent and hurt. That look he always had when he was worried about her. He was bigger now, he had filled out, was surer of himself. More of a man than when she had left. Her heart hammered inside her chest. She had no control of it. She tried to smother it with her hands so it would stop hurting. Like the day her mother left but it had been sore since. Like a pain that was deep inside it and just when you thought it was gone, something would trigger it. And now it was back. It hadn't happened to her in Doha as much. Only here, as though she was part of the land, no matter how much she tried to deny it. Her roots ran through the ground. Other people's lives here, affected hers. They belonged to her. Just as her mother had, her Amina, and well, she wouldn't say who else. It was different territory now. Instead, she would go and find Amina. Together, maybe they could go to Ramallah. She could be reminded of the pain of absence and love that Darwish spoke of in his poems. She stared outside the window of the small bedroom where she tried to grow so many of her dreams.

She left it behind and went to her favourite room in the house. The one she had secretly spent so much time in; the study full of old stories and photographs. It was as untouched as her last visit. The papers were where she had laid them out. The books still lined the shelves. Drafts and drafts of Palestinian maps of the West Bank, Gaza and Jerusalem were stacked and rolled amongst the shelves. The curtains had been left open. Outside the windows, the cypress trees stood like soldiers in rows up and down the fields. They blocked out the sky and the views and stood upright, defiant that it was even summer. Constant. Reliable. Hardy. But just in the distance, she saw a clearing. A felling of the trees. Maybe it was for a new house? Maybe new families had moved to the area, or their sons or daughters had married and come into money, and they had come home to spend it because no matter where in the world you are, home pulled at your heart to come back to it. To live amongst the memories there. To not forget the people you love, that maybe don't mean anything to anyone else in the world because they live in poor homes with few rooms and eat maybe one hot meal a week. But those people are the soldiers of this land. They are the ones that stay in the old houses and refuse to leave. They have nurtured the land for centuries, that is why the produce is blessed after years of their cultivation and hard work being poured into the soil. The blessed water that runs from their own spring in the earth. They are the ones that keep telling the stories of the families who lived before them. Of the families who are missing. They are the ones that house the children who have run out of land. Who plant seeds every year and pray for them to grow. They are the ones who have children and pray for them to grow and to stay. And some go and some come back and help them to keep building. Could Khadija be one of those who tell the stories of the missing? Her uncle's house was full of those stories, covered in dust and left abandoned like Mohammed Rasheed and others who were kept behind locked doors. She couldn't be sure of his fate, but she also didn't know if he had made it out. Yes, she would go to Ramallah and find his family. It was her mission that he did not sit behind a door amongst the piles of the missing, waiting to be found. Waiting to see if anyone loved you enough to find you, no matter where you were buried. With that in mind, she scoured through the papers. She had added her own list, her own pile of history. Her keys she took from her mother's and the note she had stuffed in her pocket when she went delivering the dresses for her mother to the families in Ramallah. She opened her locked keepsake box in which she kept her old set of keys, her mother's Quran copy and tucked within it the old piece of paper she had carefully handwritten out names and addresses on. There it was. She had recognised the name. They had made dresses for the Rasheed family and there was an old address next to the name. It was the same location in Ramallah, so it was likely it was the same family. Maybe Mohammed was their son?

Khadija set off early the next day. It was unusual to find herself following in the footsteps of her mother and Amina as she walked down to the bus stop at the edge of the village.

She hoped if she was on the first bus, she wouldn't see anyone and she could be on her way without any questions. With her uncle absent, she was glad to have her own plan. She took the bus down through the villages and into the main town towards Ramallah. There was only one road between there and Ramallah but when the Israelis blocked it off, the journey tripled in length. Thankfully, the road was unblocked. Just as the day was beginning to warm up, she arrived in Ramallah. She spent a moment getting lost in the crowds. She ordered breakfast at a café and sat watching as people walked by. On that particular day, she found herself watching a mother with a young child, about the same age she was when she came with her mother. She remembered her visit to the Mahmoud Darwish Museum and remembered the lines she repeated to herself. Absence. Her eyes followed another young couple, one baby on her hip and the father holding the hand of the other, his son. That was the reason she was there today. To find someone who she could tell about Mohammed Rasheed. She drank her coffee, wincing a bit from its strength but hoping it gave her the energy she would need to now find this person in a city of many.

She took the piece of paper and began navigating the city until she arrived at the address. She didn't recognise it but she realised that in her childhood, many things seemed bigger. There was no one there by that name, but the woman who answered knew of a Mohammed Rasheed, of an age that matched Khadija's description and she pointed to a street around the corner where the houses were falling into disrepair.

'I am sure they live there,' she said.

Khadija thanked the woman for her time. She waved it away like it was nothing but she didn't go inside. She stood at the door watching. Khadija turned around and she was leading her on, pointing to the houses further down the street. Khadija felt her watching, she had no choice but to go now, despite there being no such address on the piece of paper she had.

She knocked at the door. Loud voices shouted inside and when interrupted by her knock, they suddenly stopped. Khadija turned around and the lady was gone.

The door opened to an older man, wearing nothing but a stained vest and some long shorts.

'Yes?'

Khadija was taken aback so she stuttered slightly. 'I am looking for relatives of a Mohammed Rasheed?'

He looked at her suspiciously before answering, 'I don't know anyone by that name,' and slammed the door shut in her face. The shouting inside resumed and Khadija stood there for a moment, slightly shocked. As she turned and walked away, a woman's voice called after her. 'Wait, wait. What do you know about Mohammed?'

Khadija stopped and turned to face her. The woman was already by her side pleading with her to ignore her husband. He was suspicious because he had learnt to be and they hadn't expected him to be in any trouble, but he hadn't returned home.

'I was crossing the bridge from Doha. He was arrested at the border. I mean, I am assuming he was arrested if he hasn't come home. But he shouted out his name. Where he lived.'

'Oh, you saw him? What did he look like?'

'He was tall. His hair was thick and long. Slightly curly behind his ears.' Khadija stopped and closed her eyes, trying to

145

remember him. But she was now the only person they had that had seen this and it became important to think clearly. To relay it to his family. 'I'm sorry, it was only a moment before he was gone. I found you because he called out those details, so that's all I have to go on.'

'Where are you from?'

'The village in the hills. I had your family name because a long time ago now, my mother used to make dresses.'

'The old address was a few streets away but it became expensive to live there so we moved. But everyone still knows us,' she smiled, seeming to take solace in that.

'Yes, it was a wild guess honestly but I didn't have anything else to start with.'

'There isn't much movement here, is there? There aren't an awful lot of places for us to go anymore. 'What's your name?'

'Khadija Ahmad.'

'I think I knew your mother. Not me personally, but my mother-in-law spoke of her. Before she…'

'Yes. People also know that.' Khadija didn't really know what to say. It wasn't unusual that family names were known in Palestine. Most people knew of each other's ancestry and their family's heritage passed on and on until the present.

'It was such a tragedy. To go like that. Such a tragedy. But Allah is the Best of Planners and to Him we return.'

Khadija hadn't expected the trip to end up talking about her. Tragedy isn't the word she would have used but, in a way, she supposed it was tragic. Her mind flitted back to yesterday, to the shower room. The poor, empty house. Khadija left the family behind, feeling better that she had at least passed on his message.

***

The following days passed quickly. Every morning, Khadija was awoken by the sound of Saladin's voice. At first, it startled her. Awaking from her dreams to find his voice echoing outside the window. Each time she was pulled from her dreams, she remembered she wasn't in her apartment, alone in Doha. She was back in her childhood bed which now felt too small. Saladin's voice was close yet he was so far from her now that it all became too much. She had heard through the villagers that Amina was no longer there but she had moved down to Jericho. Others said she had left Palestine. Khadija had heard that she had family in England. Maybe she had taken her chance and left her past behind?

Khadija considered going to see what she could find. But she couldn't go down to Jericho without a car and in the summer months the drivers were fully booked, taking families on trips and excursions. She could get a bus, she thought, but where would she start? She barely knew anyone in Jericho. She came down one morning late and was surprised to see her uncle sitting stooped over in the armchair in the hallway.

'Oh, *salam* uncle. You are home then. I wondered if I was going to see you.'

'You must have made an impression in Ramallah.'

Khadija didn't answer her uncle at first, unsure of what he meant. His voice was still as harsh. He still barely moved his face to acknowledge her presence, never once looking at her in the eyes.

'A letter came. Imagine. A girl like you. A proposal.'

'What do you mean?'

'I mean your bright future must be the reason they're ignoring your past.'

Khadija's memory took her back to Taha's garden. The bird in her hands.

'I'm sorry, uncle, I don't know what you mean.'

'Isn't it obvious? The Rasheeds' boy has asked for your hand in marriage. They wrote to me,' he said waving the letter impatiently in front of her, as though the piece of paper and the air waiting between them would somehow help it to sink in.

'No, that can't be right,' Khadija said, bashfully. She felt relieved that whatever had happened to him, he must be back in Ramallah now.

'You could do worse than to marry.'

'But my studies...'

He threw the letter towards the bin. He missed but he didn't pick it up.

'I'm beyond helping you. Ever since you were young, you've done as you like.'

He walked off, leaving her behind to contemplate what had happened. She ran off to the piece of paper lying near the bin and uncrumpled it. As she read it, the words sunk in. A marriage proposal. A dowry. A new life ahead. She remembered him briefly back at the airport. He wrestled with the guards; his strong frame barely moved against the strength of four soldiers. He was a fighter. That was what Khadija wanted; a fighter. Someone who had the fire to fight back. She thought of the apartment in Ramallah. There were no orchards there. Nowhere to roam. Nowhere to pick fruit that had come from her lands and then been taken to the towns and laid out in trays among the choking city smoke. She hadn't ever considered she could live forever in a city. Would she be able to? She was in the middle of her studies and most girls her age waited until they had graduated so there was no rush to decide. Instead, she unfurled the letter and kept it aside, intending to write to them to tell them she was still a student. It was early days after all, and it was her decision, not her uncle's.

Since returning, every interaction with her uncle seemed fraught despite the fact that she had tried to be patient and happy. To be the successful traveller. The student with her international dreams laid out in front of her. But no one seemed to be as dazzled as she expected. Back home, she was just Khadija, as though she had never left. She had always been there but still in the background like a ghost that haunted her uncle's home. A wisp of a figure, floating into town, neither necessary nor needed for anyone around. She didn't provide anything to anyone. She spent most of the time avoiding people so as not to hear any news that she would carry with her when she returned. She ended up packing her clothes into her suitcase, feeling foolish for even buying them; as though dressing up would make her seem more successful, more noticeable. But it hadn't made a difference. She made a weak excuse to her uncle, who seemed to be as relieved as she was, when she told him that she had to go back to Doha earlier than expected. She felt some relief for leaving but her heart had sunk on her return and nothing had lifted her spirits. Not even the dream she told herself of her future seemed to lift her. Amina might have helped if she had tracked her down but maybe she didn't want her to and that's why she hadn't found her earlier or chased her. She also hadn't made it to Jerusalem. Although, if she was going to be honest with herself, Jerusalem seemed so far away and so completely

149

overtaken by the occupation that it scared her. From the news she had watched from when she was little when the rioting started, when Al-Aqsa Mosque was closed, she knew the city could easily descend into chaos. Images of mothers grabbing their sons, trying to tear them away from the grips of soldiers. Injured men lying on the floor, dazed and covered in blood. And that was all after they had made it through, past the towering cement walls and cattle style grids that herded Palestinians from one side to another. Stopped. Searched. Refused entry. Jerusalem was a place for the sturdy. Or for the tourists who didn't have to endure that as there was a separate side for tourists entering the city. Her green Palestinian ID card afforded her no such freedom. The ticket to Doha was her only one.

Chapter 15

WHEN KHADIJA LANDED IN Doha, she was hit first by the summer's intense searing heat. The airport was more or less empty with people choosing not to return until the latest possible dates in September to avoid the August heat. She had been told what to expect and when she arrived, she hadn't minded as much. But with disappointment weighing her down, she found it almost unbearable. But not quite as unbearable as waking up to the *athan* back home. *Is this what it takes to cure my heart?* she thought to herself, as she lugged her suitcase through to the taxi queue. She waited in the heat until a cab pulled up and she climbed into the back. The meter had already started at twenty-five dinars. She told them her address and arrived back at her small apartment, cash-less and exhausted, finding no respite in it. The air conditioning had been broken throughout the winter but the landlord had not come to fix it and she hadn't noticed too much throughout the cooler months. She switched the fridge back on and opened it to find it had been overtaken with hundreds of black ants. She left the door open and collapsed on the sofa. She lay there listening to the sound of the fridge humming back to life as the heat died down and night fell.

She awoke the next morning not feeling any better. She tidied up, swept out the ants, called the landlord to send round a technician for the air conditioning and got dressed, ready to take relief in the malls. She wandered the Venetian streets, instantly cooled by the icy chill of air conditioning. She sat down in a small café seated by the window to watch other people mill around and escape the desert heat. She pulled out her leather-bound Quran, and for want of nothing else to do, she began to read. The words reminded her of her mother and she escaped into a realm that crossed through both the living and the dead.

Weeks passed until one particular morning, she arrived at class tired from lack of sleep after a night spent between the gardens of home and the deserts of the present. The other students chatted quietly amongst themselves as they waited for Dr Reem to appear. Khadija glanced at the clock. It wasn't like her to be late. Khadija panicked. She thought it was about her grades again. She knew she hadn't really picked up since the last discussion and they had been back a few months now. She chewed the end of her pen. She flicked through her latest assignments, covered in red pen and question marks annotated at the end of her sentences as though they hadn't even made sense. A wave of nausea rippled through her stomach. The sweat around her hairline started to gather at the back of her neck. How long could she carry on like this?

When Dr Reem came in, she placed her bag down by the front desk and instead of switching on the projector, she left the students to their books and walked over to Khadija.

'I know I am not performing, I just need a bit more time and–'

'Khadija, there's a phone call for you,' Dr Reem said, interrupting her.

Khadija sat back down in her chair. 'Why? Who is it?'

'Someone from back home.'

'What is it about?'

'I think you'd better go and speak to them.'

Dr Reem hurried down the hallway with Khadija close behind her.

She saw the phone on the side of the desk. Whoever it was on the other line had been prepared to wait. Khadija was hoping she would get there and they would have hung up.

'Khadija here. How can I help?'

'Khadija Ahmad?'

'Yes, how can I help?'

'Your uncle is Jahid Ahmad?'

'Yes.'

'This is the St John's Hospital. We have been trying to get hold of you.'

'Is everything alright?'

'I'm sorry to tell you this over the phone, but Mr Ahmad has had a stroke. He has been in hospital for over a week and he is due to go home but he needs someone to care for him or he cannot be released.'

'Isn't your hospital the best place for him to stay?'

'I'm sorry, but we don't keep patients indefinitely. If there is no one to care for him in his own house, then he will be referred to the state for care.'

Khadija sat silently. Numb. The state was a death sentence.

'I'm afraid you're the closest relative we have for Mr Ahmad. There is no one else.'

153

'Ok.'

'Please call us back and advise us how you would like to proceed.'

'I will. Thank you.'

Khadija didn't know why she said thank you. Saying thank you when the last thing she wanted to do was thank them.

Dr Reem was waiting next to her. 'What are you going to do?'

'I don't know. What should I do?'

'Only you can make that decision, Khadija.'

Dr Reem left and Khadija sat motionless on the chair, watching everything continue around her. The accomplished lecturers, the brand-new halls, the flawless new books and state of the art equipment. She knew it was too good to be real for her the moment she arrived. It made sense that she wouldn't be part of this world. That she would have to return to the shadow of her childhood home, her dreams broken.

All the stories she read, the ones she heard on the news, the people coming and going from Palestine, telling stories of how they'd made it in the world outside of the Occupied Territories. She desperately wanted to be like them. To have left and become somebody else. But she knew from within the walls of her mother's home and then being a stranger inside her uncle's that she was one of those destined to stay behind in everyone else's shadow. It reminded her of her mother. How she lived within the four walls of her poor home, struggling to raise a daughter on minimal provision, minimal education and towards the end she could barely move her body. And then one day, she was gone. Is that what would become of her? The same fate, following in her footsteps. A story never fully realised. A character cast in the back, part of the unseen. Barely spoken of in case they cursed the living.

Khadija felt too angry to go and care for her uncle. The uncle who had mistreated her, who had practically abandoned her mother during her lifetime and when she needed him the most. He wouldn't continue to have a hold over her, especially in his infirmity. She awoke the next day and packed her bags, took the bus as usual, walked into class and sat down. She listened intently to Dr Reem. She left abruptly after class so she wouldn't have to answer any awkward questions. She wanted to be content with her decision. She wanted to feel that it was the right thing to do. After all, she didn't owe him anything. But on the way home, she burst into tears.

The classes became harder to concentrate in. She dreamt of her mother's home. Of monsters climbing through holes in the walls. She dreamt of Aliya and Saladin in the fields. Her nightmares followed her there. They crossed over the sea and through checkpoints. She sought temporary relief in the Venetian skyline that had been painted on the ceilings of the mall. In the anonymity of her black gowns, but it didn't fix her. After a while the mall became stale. The cracks appeared in the blue sky-coloured paint and clouds, revealing the speedy ageing of mirages in the desert. The winding gondola canals smelt of chlorine pumped in to keep the water clear and the deep blue colour wasn't real, it was simply a reflection of the chipped lagoon tiles underneath. The bridges that crossed over the canals led to nowhere. The shops sold clothes but there was nothing else to see. The food became sickly sweet, or too heavily fried and began to make her body alter. Outside, the famous Torch hotel was lit with neon colours flashing against the night-time sky, blocking out the twinkling of the stars. The incessant traffic became the backdrop to her life, unable to think because of the speed of things, the intense searing heat pounding through her. The reminders from the *athan* that vibrated through the walls of her apartment at every call to prayer reminded her what she was running from but there was no place to hide. She knew she had to return.

She spent the last week sorting her belongings, saying goodbye to those who she had befriended and those who had helped her in her hour of need. She visited the Markaz Centre and found Hiba asleep on the desk. '*Salam alaikom,*' Khadija said, noticing she had startled her. 'Sorry, I didn't mean to wake you.'

'I was sleeping here because the air conditioning is broken at home.'

'Perhaps they don't pay you enough.'

'We are volunteers here, Khadija. I ask Allah to save my palace for me in paradise. Are you ok?'

'I feel like I don't know what to do. I feel so much anger and hate towards someone who is family and I don't want to leave my future behind for him.'

'Allah looks only to your heart, Khadija. Keep it soft. Don't let the hate in the world destroy you.'

Khadija didn't speak, she just allowed Hiba's calmness to wash over her, slowly beginning to accept the inevitable. Hiba reminded her so much of her mother. They shared the same hopeful goodness that Khadija hadn't inherited. Even after the bird incident, her mother hadn't been discouraged about the state of Khadija's soul. She could see past it all and see the goodness inside. Or at least the hope that there was some good left.

Hiba left the room briefly to fetch her some water whilst Khadija read the Quran inscriptions around the room. Words of patience and goodness she had heard her mother recite to her. She had forgotten about the hope in the stories her mother had told. She had forgotten the conviction her mother had in doing what was right.

When Hiba returned, Khadija explained what had happened. She felt better for saying it out loud. Even if it was just to get a response of sympathy perhaps.

'There are many different types of people in this world. Allah made us all different with different qualities. I know that it isn't easy in Palestine. We all support Palestinians here. You are in our *duas*. You are in our prayers. But remember you are strong enough. Allah is always the Best of Planners. You need to have faith that He knows what is best for you.'

Khadija said her goodbyes and reluctantly left the Markaz Centre and the women behind. 'There are blessings in everything, Khadija. I want you to remember that,' Hiba called after her.

She would miss them and the evenings they spent there together. It was one of the few places where Khadija felt as if she did belong. As she left, she heard the storyteller's voice in her head, '*Those who gather for the remembrance of Allah will be joined by a group of angels.*' Khadija took one last look at the sisters waving to see if, amongst their sea of veils, she could see the soldiers of heaven standing by their sides.

She knew that this time she wasn't going to be returning to Doha for her studies. She had no choice but to leave the scholarship behind and Dr Reem had told her that if she missed any more school, she would be too far behind to catch up. Khadija didn't want to admit it to herself, but she was failing anyway. The information just didn't seem to sink in. Instead, her mind drifted off elsewhere. It drifted back to her home. To the upcoming weddings and harvests. It drifted off to the bustling town of Ramallah where for a brief moment she could have been a wife. It went back to the hole in the wall at her mother's house. At night, she drifted off to sleep only to be awoken by the lights on the hilltop. She knew there was something in her past she had to discover in order to move forward with her life.

She thanked Dr Reem, handed the keys back to the apartment, left the fridge door open to make it easier for the ants and left her small room in a bustling city behind her. She knew it was the end of her time there. She had felt it for a while. She packed her new clothes in a bag and dropped them off in a charity bin. With the trepidation that there was nowhere left to hide, Khadija made her way to the airport and boarded the plane back home.

***

Khadija arrived home and her uncle was in his bed. He had been transferred the day before she arrived and was being looked after by their neighbour's new daughter-in-law, Dina.

'Thank you, Dina. How has he been?'

'He doesn't move or say much. I think he will prefer you being here than me.'

'I'm Khadija by the way.'

'Oh, I know who you are. I heard many stories about you when I was growing up,' Dina said with a sweet smile. Everything about her was sweet, Khadija thought.

'Oh,' Khadija said, genuinely shocked.

'Oh, don't worry. They were all quite adventurous.'

'I'm sorry, I didn't think we had met before.'

'No, we haven't, but you know Palestinians—we all know each other from these villages.'

Khadija couldn't help noticing the silver shiny band around her finger. 'Did you get married?'

'Yes, it was our wedding in the summer. I thought you were here during the summer and would have joined everyone and come along?'

'I had to cut my trip short, so I wasn't here. Did you have a good day?'

'Oh, it was beautiful, *Alhamdulilah*. You should come over for dinner sometime now that you are back,' Dina said, her face glowing with the joy of young love.

When she stood up, Khadija noticed she held her stomach tenderly with her hands and saw the real reason for the glow in her cheeks. 'Congratulations,' Khadija said as she walked her out. She watched her delicate frame walk out the door with graceful steps. Khadija naturally pressed her hand against her own stomach and wondered what it would be like to carry life.

Her mother had never told her about her birth. Khadija wondered if that was the reason her mother had only one. Although it could have been because she was alone for all the time Khadija could remember. She had never had a father and he was never spoken about so his absence was never missed, because you can't miss someone who never existed for you.

Khadija wondered if the absence of her own birth story contributed to her feeling as though she didn't entirely exist with the living. She felt like she floated on the outskirts of being human.

A groan from the bedroom brought her back to reality and she went in to tend to her uncle. He was in bad shape. His skin was mottled yellow and damp with sweat gathering in his heavy brows.

'Khadija Hattam. Khadija Hattam. Come here.'

'It's Ahmad, uncle. You are delirious.'

He turned to look at her, his eyes squinting from the pale light coming through the window.

'Khadija. I know who it is. I am not senile.'

The days passed with minimal conversation. The days turned into weeks. Her dreams of becoming a doctor dissipated into steam from the medicine bowls. That was all she could do. She couldn't fix him. She could just care for him whilst her dreams wasted away with him. She felt empty inside, like she was wasting away. She hadn't been out much, relying mostly on Dina delivering food and although she didn't want to admit it, Saladin and his family had too. There were a few knocks at the door and she had peered outside to see him standing there but her heart ached so much, she couldn't take any more disappointment. She couldn't stand to see it opened and see Saladin. Her mind imagined him as a man standing there with his bride whilst she became a shadow in the old house. She felt as if she'd become like the stories in the archives, so she unlocked all the doors, swinging them open in defiance of her uncle's oppression. Maybe his whole life was deleting itself from his memory and his sins were burning away with his raging fever. In the quiet, lonely nights, the house seemed to breathe and echo with the ghosts from its past roaming the halls. Unlocked from the study they now drifted around, clutching keys to their old homes they could never again return to. Khadija was haunted by the images. By the gate to the garden she imagined what was behind it. Sometimes, behind it, tragedies played out. At other times it was a secret paradise. The dreams permeated her world so much that she began going out barefoot and pressing her feet into the grass to feel the life underneath her feet. She would gather plants from outside and remove seeds from the fruit, washing them down and pushing the seeds in the soil, replanting the seedlings, praying for growth and new life. Hoping that because of it, she wouldn't sink into the soil and disappear like the woman from the tale. Hoping that with their life, it would breathe new beginnings into the house and give her something to nurture.

At night when she would return to the slumber of her dreams, she woke up to him calling names of families who had lived around their neighbourhood for years but they were people she had never seen. She had kept the note from the Rasheeds. Would she want to be a wife and a mother? Would it cure her emptiness? She had learnt from her minimal experience at medical school that she couldn't fix the irrational pain in her heart. It had only intensified. She was profoundly disappointed that studying the body's physiology had revealed nothing to her.

The daytime was broken with the reality of care. It kept her so busy that sometimes she fell asleep beside his bed. She would dream of the storyteller's voice, '*An entourage of seventy thousand angels will accompany you as you visit the sick.*' Khadija sometimes thought she could feel them around her. She opened her eyes to her dreams and she could see them as described by Prophet Mohammed (peace be upon him), with outstretched wings jewelled with rubies, emeralds and diamonds surrounded by light.

'Khadija Hattam.'

'Yes, uncle, I am here,' Khadija said, snapped away from the beauty of her dreams and back to the house that had remained dark even during the bright days due to her uncle's insistence that she keep the windows and doors closed.

'Shall I fetch you something to look at from your study?'

He looked uncharacteristically alert. 'What makes you think it is my study?'

Khadija was taken aback. 'What do you mean? It is in your house of course.'

'It isn't mine. It is Salma's. It is all Salma's.'

She didn't respond, but it had distracted her. Her hands began wringing out a small flannel but she didn't realise she was dripping water in his face. He grabbed it and threw it on the floor.

'You go around like you are in another world. Away with the fairies. Just like your mother was.'

Khadija didn't answer. Just nodded mechanically from exhaustion. But she knew her mother wasn't like that. Her mother was the most logical creature she knew. She was comfortably predictable. Khadija would tell her grand stories and dreams and she would just smile at her as though her smile was telling her she loved her but she didn't understand how Khadija's mind worked.

'No, listen to me, Khadija. Your mother was exactly like you. Obstinate. A dreamer. You even look the spitting image of her.'

Khadija knew he wasn't making sense now. She was almost the complete opposite. But she smiled at him so he wouldn't get more worked up. 'Salma was a wonderful mother,' she said, not wanting to give in to his delirium but wanting to appease him because of his fragile, sick state.

'Salma was not your mother.'

Khadija sat up. A shiver ran through her body. How her uncle could be so violent, even on his deathbed. He was trying to uproot her.

'You aren't well, uncle,' she said, trying to soothe him as she became agitated. 'Quiet! We don't need to talk.'

He grabbed her wrist as a response to her outburst. It felt like a bird's ankle in his thick hands. He pulled her close to his face.

'Your name is Khadija Hattam. You are not the daughter of Salma. She was not your mother. She took you from that old woman in the street. The woman no one has ever seen or heard of since. An angel delivered you, she said; more like the devil himself. You, covered in blood. And there was Salma. Stitched you up good, she did; she never was a seamstress before you forced her hand.'

Khadija was silent. Her mind raced. Her heartbeat quickened. She shook her head.

'She gave up her life for you, this house, all her wealth, believing you were something special and I never understood why.' He shifted so he was slightly sitting up. His hand still gripped her wrist.

163

'Why do you think you don't fit with us? Have you never wondered why you are so different to her?'

'No, you are lying. It isn't true.'

Khadija could feel her blood heating up as it ran through her veins. Her uncle didn't say anything. He closed his eyes and she could see them moving about under his eyelids. She yanked her hand from his grip, now weakening in his ill health. She ran out of the room and out onto the streets. She didn't know where to go but her feet automatically took her to her mother's house. She went inside. Her eyes searching the whole time for clues to her heritage. This bare house, with its bare stone walls, couldn't possibly be hiding anything. She walked through the hole and rummaged around, expecting to find something that would reveal her past. It gave nothing up. She sat inside the damp space and cried. But the moment her eyes were shut, she saw the lights. They were vivid now. They were from the turrets up on the hilltop. She had seen the hilltop before. But from a view she didn't recognise. The house she was in. The brick wall that ran around its circumference. She went outside and traced her hand around it. Brambles and thorns had concealed most of it, but sure enough, it ran on. There was a wall. It went on for yards. It was solid. It looked like the old orchard garden walls that her neighbours had. Could it have been from the garden? She pulled over an old oil drum and stood up on it, clambering up the bramble, trying to get to the top of the wall. She climbed up it and pulled herself into the tree that was leaning on the wall. She pulled herself over and peered down. She could see an overgrown wilderness, but in the distance, a glint from a lock shone in the last rays of the afternoon sun. It was a gate. It was the same gate she had seen in her nightmares. It was the same gate she had seen in the photograph back at her uncle's house and with Saladin that day but she needed a way of getting in as it was locked shut.

Ordinarily, she would have immediately thought to go and get Saladin but due to his engagement, she knew it wasn't right. She left, resolved to go alone and was surprised when she saw Saladin on the way. She tried to avoid him, but he had already seen her coming.

'Where are you headed?'

'It doesn't matter to you,' Khadija said, hiding the photograph behind her back.

'What do we have here?' he said, smiling and darting behind her to retrieve the photograph gently from her fingertips. She didn't protest. She wanted him to see it.

'I need to go back there.'

'To the old gate we found last time?'

'Yes, I want to see what's behind it.'

'Do you want me to come?'

She nodded and her heart skipped inside. They went around to the graveyard and climbed the old cypress tree. 'You can reach the top of the wall if you climb down over here.'

'You knew all this time?' Khadija asked.

'Of a garden?' Saladin questioned. 'There are many overgrown gardens here. I remember the night we came here to the graveyard with Aliya though. Do you?'

Khadija had wanted to forget, but Saladin continued. 'Don't you remember that night, Khadija?'

Khadija looked down from the tree at the graveyard below. She shook her head.

'We turned up and you were already in the graveyard. You had been looking for the spies, waiting for Aliya to turn up and film, convinced it would be your ticket out of here and expose your uncle. Aliya was playing a practical joke on you. You two always did argue.'

'Argue? She hated me!'

'She never hated you, she told me once she wished she was as free as you.'

'What does that mean?'

'She feels all this pressure to succeed. Her whole family are counting on her to make it.'

Khadija couldn't think past her childhood. 'She lied to me.'

'You confronted her, remember? She pushed you into the soil. It's ok, I pulled you up,' he said and it made Khadija blush. She had thought of that often.

Khadija nudged him with her elbow. Saladin stood up and brushed the soil off. 'It didn't help that you were listening to the stories of the dead.'

'Now I really have no idea what you are talking about.'

'You said someone told you stories each night as a child. I think that scared Aliya the most,' Saladin was still laughing at their memories, but Khadija did not laugh. She tried to hunt through her mind. She was listening, she had assumed they had come from the walls or been carried from a neighbour's house. There was a logical explanation.

'We have storytellers. We always have.'

'The last storyteller from here?' he paused to think. 'She died years ago.'

Khadija sat still. Her. It was a woman's voice.

Her mind was racing, so Saladin carried on, 'You were only young. I've seen people around here do worse.'

'I am hardly the same. I have had it pretty easy.'

Saladin came next to her. 'Khadija, what about your scar? You have had it ever since I have known you.'

'What scar?' Khadija said, embarrassed. She didn't know anyone could see it. She thought it was always covered by her hair.

Saladin gently brushed the hair from her forehead with his finger. 'This one.'

Khadija felt where his finger had been. Beneath her hair, there was a scarred patch of skin about half the size of her forefinger.

Khadija didn't want his sympathy. She climbed down too quickly. Her hands scraped against the brick and she dropped to the ground with a thud. Saladin effortlessly climbed down into the garden. 'Let's see what we can find?' Khadija said, brushing herself off. She wasn't looking for the garden; she was looking for the gate. It led into the back near the second building. 'Why is it bricked off? Why didn't we use it when I was young?'

'You wouldn't have seen it, hidden by all this growth,' Saladin said, still trying to clear the overgrowth surrounding them. The garden was dark so they could barely make anything out.

But they were forced to duck down. The light had fallen. Dusk brought with it the lights from the hilltop. They were shining now and with every rotation they shone into the garden, lighting it up like it was the middle of the day.

'That's why,' Saladin said and they ran under the cover of darkness away from the light's beam and back to the streets. 'It is like any of the other abandoned gardens and orchards around here.'

'Except, it's mine.'

'But what do you expect to find there?'

'The truth, something about what happened when I was a child. I see this place sometimes in my nightmares.'

Saladin scanned their surroundings. 'We have to go, Khadija. And I will be expected at home.'

'Yes, of course, you will be,' she said, letting him leave so she didn't have to hear any more news of his home than she had to. As they climbed the wall, she glanced at the gardens as they alternated between light and dark. They looked as if they could have been magnificent once.

Chapter 16

KHADIJA'S UNCLE PASSED SOON after his revelation. His funeral came around. As was customary, most of the neighbours came and Khadija greeted them on their arrival. Aliya came. Khadija tried not to let the sting of their old rivalry appear obvious on her face but her eyes couldn't help searching to see if Saladin was close by. She couldn't see him. The chapter *Yassin* was read as the mourners silently listened. When the burial was over, Khadija was left staring at the pile of mud that covered him. She didn't realise she had been standing there for so long. When her thoughts did come back to the present, she realised she was alone and dusk was almost upon her.

Khadija went back to her uncle's house. Sadness flooded in as she closed the door behind her. But it shifted ever so slightly when she realised the house was hers to do whatever she wished with now. The rooms no longer belonged to her uncle. The solicitor had told her as much. He said he would do some investigating but that her uncle had survived his only sister and that Khadija was the legal owner of both of their inheritances.

The next morning, the first thing Khadija did was go into the downstairs library and pull open the old heavy curtains blocking the windows. The light streamed in, making her feel more satisfied. She walked through the hallway and up the stairs until she reached the left wing and proceeded to open all the doors, curtains and windows. The light lit up the dust clouds in the room that were disturbed from her walking through them. The light fell on the pile of articles and photographs. She flicked through them, daunted by the task of organising generations of lives.

She woke early the next day and the house seemed to breathe with relief to have a dawn opening it up and cracking through the gloom that had overcome it. Khadija was up just before the brightness of the sun and she thought of her mother, Salma. She thought of her praying before *fajr*. She turned on the tap in her small sink, washed and prayed just before the sun rose fully. Shortly afterwards, she dressed and decided to begin clearing out her uncle's room. However, when she opened his wardrobes and saw they contained five or six suits and little else, she closed the door and spent a few moments in the surreal realisation that they would stay there. Unworn. But there was something else at the back of his wardrobe. A parcel she recognised. She remembered back to when she arrived at her uncle's house. She was sure it was Amina who had left a parcel at the door. Khadija had never opened it and there it was in front of her; the tin her uncle had taken stuffed at the back of his wardrobe gathering dust. She was sure the parcel might be able to tell her more. She unwrapped it so eagerly she tore the binding around it. A book fell out onto her lap. It was a copy of the Quran. She opened the pages until she reached a personalised bookmark ribbon, inlaid with Amina's initials on. She had bookmarked the chapter, The Cave. It was a chapter her mama would often recite to her too. Maybe that was why? She looked inside the pages at the beginning and end for notes, a revealed secret, but there was only a note saying she was going to Jericho for the time being and she enclosed the address of her apartment there. Why would Amina have left the Quran for her? She had copies in the house. She had to find Amina. Amina would know the truth. She left the house behind her and headed to the bus station to make the journey down to Jericho.

Khadija knocked at the door of the address she was given. The glass-fronted, concrete apartments rose four storeys high. The ground floor one she was stood at had a pretty decorated courtyard out the front just slightly set back from the street and road. But it was a quiet area. The houses were mostly traditional one-storey villas, some hadn't been altered in decades, or even centuries, Khadija thought, looking at the small metal barred windows looking out onto generous courtyards, gardens and farms that sprawled out behind them. Jericho was hotter than where she lived. It was a valley beneath mountains, lined with old date palm trees, orange trees producing fruits the size of grapefruits and an air that smelt of jasmine during its evenings. Where Khadija was standing, there was a small courtyard garden and a table and two chairs looking out onto the street. The street was old. The roads were barely more than trampled down stone. There were no notable pavements and the shops to the right of the apartment blocks had been there for decades too.

After a few minutes, the door opened. Amina looked older than Khadija had remembered her. She flung forward and embraced her. 'Khadija, look at you, so grown up.'

'I've missed you, Amina.'

'Come in, come to the kitchen. We will make some tea. We have a lot to talk about.'

Khadija followed her into the open-plan apartment. She had a large kitchen that overlooked a sitting area with horizontal windows at one end. They gave her a view out over to the older houses on the opposite side of the street.

'So, how is Doha? Are you enjoying it?'

'How did you know? I couldn't find you before I left.'

'I asked after you, often. And well, exciting news of a village girl winning a scholarship in Doha was spoken about amongst everyone and I was thrilled for you.'

'I am back for good now. I had to care for uncle before he died.'

Amina stopped making tea and began to fiddle with the tie on her apron. 'So why will you not return?'

'I've missed too much. My scholarship has been cut.'

'Oh Khadija, I'm sorry. I have some money. Maybe I can–'

'No, Amina, I am fine, thank you. I am not sure being a doctor was exactly suited to me. Plus, I have a lot to sort here.'

'Like what?' Amina said tentatively as she brought over a tray of tea and dates.

'My childhood home. My uncle's house.'

'You are living at your uncle's?'

'Yes… for the time being,' Khadija said, glancing around at the apartment. How homely and inviting it was only intensified how she felt about returning to her uncle's house, that it induced tears.

'Oh Khadija, what is the matter?'

'I hate the house, Amina. I hated it from when I was small and I don't want to live there but I have nowhere else to go.'

'You have your mother's old house.'

'It has fallen into disrepair. I doubt it is even safe. A wall inside has been broken in half and I don't know how safe the roof is anymore.'

Amina dropped her tea glass. It smashed on the floor. 'Are you ok?' Khadija asked, watching Amina as her hands shook, trying to pick the pieces up. 'What is it, Amina? Tell me. I know you know something.'

'That wall was put up to protect you, Khadija. Salma arranged for it to be built the day after you arrived.'

'I stepped inside it. I thought it was a safe room or somewhere you could hide if the soldiers ever came.'

'No, it wasn't made for that.'

'Does it have anything to do with what uncle told me just before he died?'

Khadija could tell by the paleness that had flooded Amina's face that he had been telling the truth.

'Amina, please. I deserve to know.'

'I assume what he said was that Salma wasn't your mother, Khadija, not by birth but believe me, she was ever since. You had become an orphan, Khadija. Salma made her decision quickly and took you in as her own. No one ever spoke of it again so you could have as normal a life as possible. Only a handful of us ever knew. I wanted to tell you back when your uncle came but he had designs on the house. He wanted it for himself so he took you to ensure he got it. But things didn't work out by the sounds of it.'

As Amina was talking, she wondered if she meant the keys Khadija had that she had taken from her mother's house all those years ago. She had taken them from her mother's bedside automatically on leaving with a handful of her other belongings. The keys weren't usually out. Why had her mother taken them out? Was she going to tell her that morning?

'I have the keys. I think that's what she wanted to tell me. She had the keys out, but I never thought anything of it.'

'There is a lot for you to discover now you have your uncle's estate and your old home. Why don't you stay here? You look tired. Get some rest. You can stay with me as long as you want and we can work it out together. I have to leave now to visit Sidu Naser opposite. He is on his own now and he has his dinner at this time. Well,' she said, glancing at her watch, 'I am actually late so he will be wondering where I am.'

'Sidu Naser?'

'He is one of the oldest men in the village so I help him with a few things, as and when I can. You can take his dinner round one day if you like? I think he would enjoy some company for a while as I often don't have the time to chat as much when I am on my delivery rounds.'

Khadija nodded her head in agreement, not fully registering because of the shock and relief she felt. Shock because what her uncle had said was true, but relieved because she didn't have to go back to his house. She imagined their dark ominous walls and how they sucked the daylight out. She preferred to be here, in Amina's cosy apartment, decorated with paintings of Palestine's famous landscapes. The long lounging sofa underneath the window that gave a view of old flat-roof houses and in the distance, the striking backdrop of the mountains that wrapped around the town. Even the air was balmy and the palm trees wavered in the slight breeze. Jericho was a happier place for her than home. She didn't see any reason for her to rush back. She curled up on the sofa exhausted and fell asleep.

Amina arrived back, waking her up with a bowl of soup that reminded Khadija of her childhood, the happier parts before the dead sheep. They sat and talked throughout the evening, moving out onto the courtyard with their late-night mint tea brewing in a glass pot. They spoke of Salma and their times together. Amina told her about why she left all those years ago. She felt threatened if she had dared to open her mouth any more than she had on the day he came to claim guardianship of her. So, Amina moved back to her apartment in Jericho. The morning before she left, she left the parcel and a note on the doorstep. Khadija told her how she hadn't opened it until recently when she had discovered it again amongst her uncle's things.

'You were the orphan, Khadija, but I wanted to remind you that you didn't need anyone except Allah, no matter how desperate it felt. And it must have done when you had to go and live with your uncle. Forgive me. I felt powerless. That offering was all I had to give you. Did you know why I chose the chapter, The Cave?'

'I am starting to see, yes. In the story, there is an explanation about treasure hidden underneath a wall. The wall is rebuilt, concealing the treasure but it is revealed that it is being protected until the orphans come of age. My mother used to recite it to me often.'

'Yes, that's right. It kept her calm knowing that even though it looked bleak, the orphans in the story were cared for. It gave your mother, Salma, comfort through those long hard days and nights that even in the absence of your parents, you were being taken care of. And after her, well it became a comfort to me.'

They spoke until the moon was high in the sky and they both decided to get some sleep. They had years to catch up on but they felt they had time in which to do it, so there was no rush. And reminiscing about the immediate past that they both shared was more comforting for Khadija than revealing anything further back. She knew there must be more, but she also didn't want to overburden her. She knew with time, it would be revealed but for now, she needed the strength to deal with life. She needed to recover day by day and to find herself before she had the strength to find out what her future looked like. She had been absent of companionship for so long that she didn't want to ruin it with nightmares of the past. That was the first night of many that she slept soundly.

It was only on the second week that she awoke with a start. It was the same sound that rumbled through her subconscious and rattled into the conscious. She had heard it before. Like the dull rumble of an earthquake trembling through the streets. But the sound was not from the centre of the earth or the tectonic plates underneath it. The sounds were only streets away. Khadija ran to the window. Amina followed after in her dressing gown as she wrapped her headscarf around her hair.

'Come away from the window, Khadija.'

'I'm not a child anymore, Amina,' Khadija answered, staring at the tanks rolling down the streets. Her heart began beating, as fast as a bird's heart.

Can't you remember, little girl? The shots rang out. He lay there on the floor bleeding. A woman ran over and covered him, another bang rang out and her screaming stopped. She had a blanket of dark black curls just like you, Khadija.

You ran through a winding alleyway cut between the two houses as your heart pounded in your chest. Faster than the bird's heartbeat. Your feet ran so fast they nearly tripped over themselves until you reached a stranger in the streets. You never did see her again. Your angel in human form illuminating those dark streets.

Salma was at home but she was walking through the streets that evening after Isha prayer. She wanted a longer walk and something pulled her towards the end of town. And there she found you in the arms of a woman she had never seen before. But you were bleeding, she took you and ran to her house to help you, assuming that the woman would follow but when she turned around, she had gone. After she had tended to your cut, her brother, who was the only family she had left, told her to leave her family home if she made the choice to keep you as her own. So, she had only one place she could take you and it was the old quarters of your estate. She had the house locked up and the alleyways blocked at either end. She never wanted you to see them or to walk through them and be reminded of what you saw that day. But it was always your destiny to see. Just not until you were strong enough. You are strong enough now, Khadija.

Khadija replayed the flashback in her mind. It was true. The nightmares were interchangeable. The lights on the hilltop from the tanks rolling down the hill. The army base at the top of the hill. Her family home; the ruins she had walked around. The gate she had passed through; that's why it was familiar. Because it was her home before they were gone. Khadija thought that when she was ready, she would return to the gardens and the bricked-up house and she would uncover the truth. The final piece of her locked behind gardens that had grown into a wilderness, waiting to be uncovered.

Chapter 17

IT WAS ONE EVENING when Khadija packed up the food Amina made and prepared it to take to Sidu Naser. Sidu Naser was called Sidu, not because of a grandparent relationship, but out of respect as he was the oldest man in the village. Khadija was happy to help. It was the least she could do, she thought. Some old plaster fell from the cracks above as she knocked on his door. She glanced around the courtyard. The stone wall that was once solid and half the height of the street lamps had begun to disintegrate. Sidu Naser opened the door, squinting from the daylight now flooding into his small hallway.

'*Salam alaikom*, who is this?'

'*Wa alaikom salam,* Sidu Naser. It is Khadija. I am bringing food from Amina.'

'Come in. Sit, sit. So, your mother is...?'

'Salma. I am Salma's daughter. We lived just outside of Ramallah in the countryside.'

'Ah yes, I know now,' Sidu Naser said, beckoning her to sit in the chair as she unpacked the food onto the old dining table.

'Did you know my mother, Sidu Naser?' Khadija said, not wanting there to be any awkward silences.

He looked at her, his eyes narrowing slightly as if he was unsure of how to answer the question. So, Khadija made it clearer for him, 'My birth mother.' Saying it out loud didn't make it sound any more real. But she blurted it out. It was all she had been thinking about. Sidu Naser sat with his hands clasped together. His breathing was heavy and laboured from his old age. He sat for a few minutes, rocking gently back and forth before he spoke.

'There are many like your mother, Khadija, and your father, may Allah bless their souls. It is the price we pay for living here.' His eyes seemed to look into his past. She knew that he must have seen so much of life. He placed his steaming hot tea cup on the tray and poured her some sweet mint tea in a delicate glass. The sugar scented the steam with its sticky sweetness and she wasn't sure she could stomach it.

'You know we all have our stories, Khadija. I feel like I am bursting with them. I heard of what happened to your parents. These villages and towns are all connected. What happens to one family, is shared amongst us so it happens to us all. But yes, your parents, they were good people. They had a beautiful property, a vast orchard and farms.' He reached for his tea, so Khadija leaned forward quickly and handed it to him to save him moving out of his chair that had shaped around the curve of his back. He leaned back with a sigh. 'Some say it was a rogue soldier. Others say it was a campaign so they could divert the water that ran through the grounds.'

'What do you say?'

'Allah knows best.'

'Do you think they were looking for me? After I escaped that night?'

Sidu Naser looked intently at her and grabbed her hands. His skin felt as soft as butter. 'Do not fear them, Khadija. Or anyone else for that matter. Allah is the Owner of Power. Not them, with all their guns and weapons. Have faith that He knows what is best. You are protected every minute of the day. Every second, in fact. Live your life.'

'Is that why Salma changed my surname to hers?'

'Yes, it was. She was nervous. She was scared. As a young girl you had seen so much. Salma ordered the house to be bricked up to close it off. She didn't want you stumbling through the gate, or soldiers finding you and taking you, or worse.'

'What about now?'

Sidu Naser waved his hand in front of his face, dismissing the notion.

'What about the house? I heard that it was structurally unsound?'

'No, Khadija, it isn't. It was one of the most finely built houses I have ever seen. Oh, if only it could be restored to how it was. I should love to go back there.' Naser's eyes glanced off to the distance to some image of the past.

'Jahid wanted the house. That's why, I'm guessing he told you, you couldn't go there. Do you know he started having work done?'

Khadija shook her head and walked over to the window. 'Wait, there was a hole inside the walls. I wondered what that was.'

'Yes, I imagine his plan was to take the whole estate back.'

'The whole estate?'

'It used to stretch from the street to the hilltops.'

Khadija wondered if that was the real reason he packed her off to Doha in the first place. She had started going through his things and she had been back to the old house just before he sent her away. Khadija came back from the window and sat down. She imagined the forbidden golden fields rolling towards the hilltops, the paved courtyards, the length of the brick wall and the once magnificent gardens inside it.

'Why didn't he go through with it?'

'There were many reasons. Cursed, that's what a lot of the folk said. He had taken it from you and no matter how hard he tried to break down those walls, he was plagued with issues. I am not sure I believe that old tale, but something must have happened inside there because he locked it up and didn't return. Then, he fell ill. And you know the rest.'

'I had no idea.'

'Why would you? You don't know him. He wasn't a bad man, Khadija, but wealth is a hard thing for some to resist.'

Khadija felt on the brink of tears. Tears of frustration and injustice. She had separated herself from her past for so long and even when she left Palestine behind, she couldn't leave it as she imagined. 'Sidu, let me take this to the kitchen,' she said, scooping up the drinks tray and almost dashing off to the kitchen. It was a narrow strip of a kitchen with pots piled on either side in need of washing. A small window looked out onto the courtyard but thick metal bars obstructed most of the view. She slid on a pair of washing up gloves and began scrubbing the week-old dishes. She grabbed the bowls, scrubbed them clean and piled them on the draining board. Afterwards, she dried them all and stacked them in orderly lines in the cupboards. She wiped the sides down and opened the window. It allowed a little push outwards to have some air seeping through. The daylight barely entered but she was glad for the cool shadows that hid her in those moments. She wept because if there was anything scarier than a life enslaved by occupation, it was one of growing old in it. She wept because Sidu Naser's house was poor. Because time ravaged itself even worse in areas where goods and materials were hard to come by and money even harder. Where you would survive so much and then leave the earth behind, leaving your home and gardens crumbling into their foundations. She thought of the woman sinking into the soil. How long would it be before everything she knew would be lost and his house buried under years of sand and time?

She thought of her parents. She thought of the photographs her uncle had. How the farms and gardens were beautifully lush and fertile, how she could barely remember them.

All those thoughts she had had of Salma not being ambitious enough. Of not leaving the place and people behind, without Khadija realising that would have meant she wouldn't have had a home. She didn't realise her poverty was a choice in order to protect her because she would never take the wealth of an orphan, instead dedicating her life to raising her in hardship. How she wished she could thank her and tell her now she was beginning to understand her sacrifices. She remembered the morning she left. She remembered she didn't have time for her.

'Khadija, what's the matter?' Sidu Naser had appeared at the doorway on his walking sticks. His trousers creased around the knees, held up by a pair of braces.

'Salma, I let her down,' Khadija sobbed.

'Don't be sad, dear. There is plenty you can do for Salma now.'

'What do you mean?'

'A child making *dua* for a parent that is gone. You are alive, my dear. You have one thing that they don't have and I have very little of.'

'What?'

'Time, *in'shaa'Allah.*'

They were interrupted by the sound of Amina coming through the door. Amina beckoned for Khadija to leave with her. She kissed Sidu Naser's hand, thanked him for the tea and left.

'I feel sad for him.'

'Why?' Amina said, startled.

'His house, he doesn't have much.'

'Oh Khadija, I don't think you understand what it is he truly values. It isn't in the shiny and new. It is in the eternal.'

Just as they were approaching the door of the flat, Amina stopped. 'Do you know who owns this?' Amina said, pointing to her building. Khadija shook her head, so Amina continued. 'His sons. They own the whole building. They have saved the top floor for him. It is a brand new three-bedroom apartment with views all over the town.'

'Well, why doesn't he move?'

'That is his home, Khadija. Why would he want to?'

They stepped inside and Khadija went to rest on the sofa. She thought much of everything around her and slowly things were beginning to look different.

Over the coming weeks, she began to establish a routine in Jericho. She loved visiting town each morning to buy fresh fruit. She would pick up a falafel pitta, pickle and fresh bread. She preferred to go early to the market when traders were out on the streets delivering their goods in the town centre. That way she would spend time browsing and selecting the freshest of produce that was there the earliest. It was just as her mother had said, the best fruit on earth.

By the time she was finished, it was midday prayer time at the blue dome mosque that sat in front of a river, with the mountain's peaks behind it. Sometimes the peaks faded in the clouds and haze, other times they were sharp and imposing. The *muezzin*'s voice was so unlike Saladin's but it didn't stop her from thinking of him or what he was doing. Her mother had always been so proud of her praying on time, that she felt it would be some consolation to eradicate the bad thoughts that had slowly crept into her mind. She spent time asking Allah to help her. After all, He had her entire life without her even realising.

In the afternoons, she helped Amina prepare dinners. The old recipes reminded her of her childhood, and day by day she learnt the techniques from Amina and they were similar to what her mother made. She learnt how to boil the meat or chicken in a stock flavoured with cardamom, black pepper, onions and seasoning. She learnt how to cut and slice the okra, frying in a deep pan of golden oil before lifting it out, and laying it on the kitchen roll as she cut tomatoes and added puree and smashed pieces of garlic to make the traditional *bamia* dish with okra, tomatoes and lamb. She combined the strained stock with the fried garlic and coriander leaves, added the tomatoes and puree and simmered with the okra. When it had stewed, it was served with the lamb over freshly cooked rice.

'We can't always get lamb, it is so expensive now, so you can do this just with okra, or with chicken or beef. The key to being a Palestinian chef is to use what you have at your disposal,' Amina reminded her.

They sometimes had lamb during the celebration of Eid Al-Adha. It was the sacrifice and lambs were slaughtered and their meat distributed amongst the community. Khadija hadn't eaten lamb since she saw the dead sheep on the day that had changed it all. She couldn't stomach it. But the dish was just as delicious with okra and no meat.

After a few weeks, Khadija had mastered most of the basic recipes Amina had taught and she relished cooking for hours, especially when it was to feed others. A particular memory was brought back by a dish of her childhood. *Mussakhan* was the dish of her hometown, flavoured with the red sumac spice, ground from the trees that grew wild there. Freshly ground sumac, cumin and cinnamon mixed with olive oil, salt and pepper. Amina taught her how to quarter the chicken and roast it on a baking tray, taking care to keep the juices. She pan-cooked the onions with more spices and then assembled the chicken, onions and some local nuts (Khadija remembered that her mother had used almonds), and she grilled all until the bread crisped up. It was pulled out of the oven, and shared. With each mouthful, a happier childhood of Khadija's emerged. She wasn't entirely sure how many days of them she had experienced, but they were the ones that she wanted to keep and remember. She repeated this process of cooking *Mussakhan* until it became second nature to her. Each time she shared and ate the dish, she was reminded of where she came from.

The vine leaves were picked each summer and frozen flat in the freezer to be used all year round. They were taken out and defrosted and laid flat. Then, uncooked fat grains of short rice, tomatoes and herbs were skilfully placed inside as Amina wrapped them effortlessly, closing the leaves around it whilst

Khadija lagged behind, her fingers fumbling over the delicate art.

'How do you do it so fast?' Khadija laughed.

'Years of practice. You will get there, just keep going!'

The smell of the grapevine leaves filled the room as the steam poured from the steamer. The once tough vine leaves were now silky soft and served in the sticky sauce they were cooked in. A mound of them on a plate was enjoyed for dinner and throughout the day for the next meal, and portions were delivered to the neighbours.

Khadija had time to read more. She began to apply her knowledge from the Markaz Centre and began reading classical Arabic in the Quran again. Amina told her to read the story she had saved for her all those years ago and so, she began with that one. Slowly deciphering the word and the meanings behind it. The orphans. The treasure. The wall. It was so like her circumstances but she had been too melancholic and misled to see it. So, with this new perspective, she began to see things alter and change. As though she was given a new lease of life. Now, although her steps and plans were unknown, they had hope. And that was something she hadn't felt in a long time.

Amina sat with her one evening and pulled out a basket of material. She handed it to Khadija. 'Do you remember this?' Khadija looked at the material on a dress, half-finished. Poor, uneven stitches had been added underneath perfectly formed stitches. It was a pattern she had seen before.

'Was this mine and my mother Salma's?'

'Yes,' said Amina, 'I was trying to help her to get some sewing done before it happened. She used to sell them to make some sheikals.'

'Yes, I remember. I also tried to take it over when she was ill but I never did finish learning. And look, you can see how bad my stitching was!'

'Sit with me then, I can show you. We can finish the *thowb* she was working on. This one was for you anyway.'

Khadija held it up and laughed. 'I don't think it would fit anymore.'

'You are too grown up for it now. But who knows, maybe one day you can give it to your daughter.'

Khadija stopped and dropped the blue thread on the floor. 'This is why she went to the market that day, when they came. It was to buy me the thread because I wanted to stitch the colour of the sky.'

Khadija broke down in tears on Amina's lap.

'It isn't your fault, Khadija. What Allah wills happens. Your mother would have done anything for you and may Allah reward her with Paradise for it now.'

'*Ameen*,' Khadija said, composing herself. '*Ameen*.'

Amina showed her the basic patterns that she was creating on the dress. They began with the cypress tree and Khadija imagined they were mountains.

Chapter 18

ON ONE OF HER morning walks back to the flat, a cool breeze enveloped the town and carried the sand in the air with it and half-hid the mountains in its haze. Khadija saw Amina making her way towards her with some determination.

'Khadija, I am glad I found you. You have a visitor at the flat.'

'Who?'

'Saladin.'

'How does he know I am here?'

'I saw one of my old friends from Ramallah in town and I told her I had a visitor. News travels fast here.'

'No, I can't come and see him.'

'What do you mean?'

'Amina, I can't. Not after everything that's happened.'

'What are you talking about, Khadija?'

'Aliya and him.'

'You really must stop listening to rumours.'

Despite protesting the whole way, Amina took her home, insisting that she wouldn't have him waiting whilst she sauntered around town. He had travelled from the northern part, her old town, and if they closed the checkpoint before nightfall, he wouldn't be able to get back.

Saladin was waiting outside on the table and chairs that sat just outside Amina's block of flats in a communal courtyard. He stood up immediately as he saw Khadija coming down the street with Amina's arm hooked in hers.

'I will just drop the shopping inside,' Amina said, opening the door and leaving Khadija to go and greet Saladin.

'How are you?' he asked, in that voice that she had heard so often.

As he stood there, he reminded her of the boy who had lifted Salma off the floor when she had fallen. Of the boy who had lifted her from the soil in the graveyard.

'*Alhamdulilah*, I am good here. Thanks. How are you?'

'*Alhamdulilah*,' he said, followed by a silence that hung awkwardly between them.

'How can I help?' Khadija said, more formally than she would have liked, but her voice was off; it kept breaking and swaying under the pretence of being normal.

'Well, I have asked Amina. And she agreed. So, with her being your only guardian left... I wanted to give you this.'

He thrust a letter into her hand and practically dashed off down the street. Khadija had received letters before. Probate, inheritance. Did people want to rent her uncle's and now her house as she wasn't there? Had her solicitor been in touch? She wasn't ready to open it and deal with the grown-up world quite yet so she ran inside to Amina.

'I was just about to bring out some juice and fruit,' Amina said.

'He has gone, Amina.'

'Oh. Well, maybe he had to rush back. Will you follow him shortly?'

Her comment threw Khadija off.

'Don't you want me here?'

'Don't be silly. I love having you here. But you are a young woman now, Khadija. It is time you began to build your own future.'

'I like it here, though.'

'I like you here too, but Jericho isn't the place that haunts you.'

Khadija watched as Amina collected her grocery bags and after hearing a little here and there about dinner preparations, she left the flat. Khadija couldn't stay in after her. She needed to get some air. To think. She saw the mountain ranges in the distance and walked towards them. She walked through the streets that led to Temptation Mountain. On the outskirts of one of the oldest archaeological sites in the world, Temptation Mountain stood as its backdrop. *This is where Jesus hid from the devil for forty days and forty nights.* Behind the natural cave system, halfway up the mountain, there was now a monastery. In front of the monastery was a café providing refreshments to worshippers and tourists. The café had the best view out of Jericho. And it was so far up the mountain range, that it felt miles away from the town. It was the perfect place for Khadija to go to gather her thoughts. She passed up through the archaeological site. She stared down at the ruins and the pegs of what was left of the ancient city that existed well before her and wondered what else the land underneath her feet hid. She glanced up to the lights on Temptation Mountain and began to climb until she reached the café.

She ordered a cold glass of the famous Jericho orange juice and sat down, looking at the valley below her. She knew Amina was right. Her nightmares broke through into the daylight. The ruins of her past still lay half-buried under the rubble. Maybe it was time to go back.

She opened the letter, ready to deal with the legalities inside. She opened it up and was surprised to see it was handwritten, in writing she recognised from her school days. As she read through its contents, she was glad she was on her own so no one was there to see the happiness that dared to show itself so openly on her face. She knew she must return home and the letter she had only made her more intent upon it. She replied to the letter and gave it to a family who Amina had heard were travelling to the north and were more than happy to deliver it.

Over the following days, Amina packed Khadija some of her favourite things from Jericho. Khadija finished off her *tatreez* and finalised the last few recipes that had eluded her since childhood. On the last day, Khadija thanked Amina for being there for her when no one else was and told her she would come to visit her soon. Before she took the bus home, she stopped in to say *salam* to Sidu Naser.

'*Salam alaikom*,' she said, peering round at him sitting on the courtyard, warming his face in the sun. 'How are you?'

'*Alhamdulilah*, I am here another day.'

Khadija said her goodbyes and boarded the bus that would take her home. She walked back to her uncle's house just as dusk was approaching. The temperature was considerably lower than Jericho's and she was relieved to get inside. She placed her bags in the hall and went upstairs to his old study and took out the images of the gardens and farms that were adjacent to her family's original home. Around one of the bird's-eye views, there was a marking in red pen all around its circumference.

191

She gathered her papers and placed the rest of the paperwork in a lockable cabinet at the end of the room. She had an idea to deliver it to Palestinian university library archives so it would be accessible to anyone. Salma had spent her life piecing it together before Khadija had appeared and soon it would no longer be in the locked rooms of an old Palestinian house. She needed to help others piece together their history and events so that they could be recorded and kept in archives where they might mean something one day. In the meantime, she needed the circumference of her old property legally mapped out and the inheritance sorted for her uncle's property.

Over the next couple of weeks, she began to clear her uncle's house. She borrowed a car from Dina next door and delivered cupboards full of clothes, blankets and stores to a local charity for refugees. She kept some select books and furniture but mostly, because it reminded her of her past, she arranged for it to be taken and given to families that needed them. As she packed his grotesque creature figurines, one dropped on the floor and smashed. The label underneath was of a store for tourists. The figurines had come no further in the world than Jerusalem. Underneath them, was a locked old drawer. She took the bunch of keys off the nearby bookshelf until she found the small brass key that opened it. Inside, her uncle's last secret was revealed. A stack of payslips had been stored away. She read through a few, shortly realising that all of them were the same. His business had been to seek employment at an Israeli factory. That was his secret.

Nearing the end of the second week, the house was a shell. It was a decent-sized property, with an amiable-sized front garden with a solid tree and a hardy lawn. She was pleased that her work had turned it into a place that could now be a home for a family who would fill its bedrooms and tread down the lawn with visitors and clean its windows and open its curtains every morning. She was content because there would be life inside it. Just not hers.

***

The days that followed were shaping up to be the happiest since she received the news in Saladin's letter.

After Saladin had sought permission from Amina, he had delivered the letter laying out his intended proposal of marriage to Khadija. It read that after his father's retirement, he was to take over Imam duties at the mosque in their hometown. If she would say yes, he would be happy that he was finally answering her initial proposal when she was too young to ask. She couldn't believe that she might be so close to realising this long-held dream of hers.

She had accepted with her heart singing a happiness it had never felt before. It was the marriage proposal she had longed for. He had never been engaged to Aliya. He didn't even know about this particular tale and Khadija didn't say any more, wondering if it was a last attempt of her uncle's to hurt her. But with him gone and her future laid out in front of her, she didn't have an ounce of sadness in her heart. It was too full of joy. Dina came over to visit her uncle's house.

'Well, Khadija, how are the plans going? Do you need any help?'

'I haven't done much at all, Dina. But I did find this,' Khadija said tentatively, handing over a black and white photograph of her parents on their wedding day.

193

'I recognise the fields. They are next to your old home.'

Khadija smiled and answered her first question, 'I am sure I will be fine. It is just going to be a small ceremony.'

'Oh, come on, I love arranging weddings.'

The wedding seemed too surreal. She threw herself into sorting her uncle's house out instead. It was tangible. Real. But the wedding and life after, well that was something completely different. Just as they were talking, Khadija heard a voice behind her on the lawn. She turned around to see Saladin's mother, Umm Farooq, with Saladin's two older sisters, Farooq and Fatima, smiling at her from each side of their mother. They were only a year older than her but they seemed younger in their demeanour than she ever did.

'*Salam alaikom*, Khadija.'

Khadija answered and then turned to Dina who was already making excuses to leave. Dina left on the promise that she would see her soon to help her with the wedding plans.

'Do you want to go inside?' Khadija said, as they stood on the grass.

'No, out here is just fine,' Umm Farooq said, sitting down in an empty chair with the girls dragging theirs next to Khadija.

'Please let us help!' the girls piped in. Their mother looked at them and smiled. 'What can I say, they have been very excited and won't hear that you won't accept our help. After all, we will all be family soon.'

Khadija went inside to fetch some lemonade and fruit.

'Where will the wedding be?'

'Will it be here or will you go somewhere bigger, like the hall in Jericho near Temptation Mountain?'

'Or, there are many wedding halls in Ramallah. That's where I would choose.'

'Calm down, girls. Khadija, I'm sure, has her own ideas.'

'I wondered about staying local. In the fields here, close to where my parents were married.' Khadija paused.

'A field!' gasped the twins, in sync.

Khadija was relieved when Umm Farooq interrupted, 'I think it is a fine idea. A traditional wedding in your home-town. I love the idea.'

Khadija realised she had been holding her breath and ex-haled deeply when she had won her mother-in-law's approval. They discussed some details and an expected date that wasn't too far ahead, as they were keen to catch the last few weeks of good weather before an outdoor wedding would become impossible and would have to be delayed until next spring. It didn't give them much time to plan, but Umm Farooq said they would take care of the food, seating and decorations. Khadija said it was too much, but she brushed it off, eager to help and to have the girls have something productive to do in the last few weeks of their holidays as they had spent much time getting into mischief or not doing much at all.

The days followed in a blur of wedding plans, flower choosing, menu planning and at last, the wedding dress. An evening of henna was arranged with Umm Farooq leading the bridal party, dressed in their embroidered dresses through the town to collect Khadija at her house. Khadija loved that the room was full of soon-to-be family and delicious treats, and sat observing it all unfold around her as the girls decorated her skin with henna. They spent the evening singing songs of their future happiness and dreams. Khadija slept and that night, she dreamt of children running through her fields of gold.

They awoke the next morning for their shopping trip to Ramallah. The girls roamed the bridal boutiques until Khadija found a satin white dress that was a simple, unfussed design like the one her mother wore in her photographs. Khadija pulled one of the photographs out of her pocket that she had found in her old childhood home. It was of her parents' wedding day. She studied the intricate *tatreez* on her mother's dress as best as she could using the worn image. She recognised some of the patterns. She would love to find the same, but it wasn't as easy now and it was very expensive. She looked at the plain dress and thought she might be able to stitch her own design. She didn't have much time but from what Amina had taught her, she could stitch a memory to her mother, even if it was just adorning the veil.

The twins were eager for her to try on a few hundred designs but Khadija was adamant this was the one she wanted now she knew that she was going to try and work on it before the wedding. The girls flicked through the rails, pressing dresses up against their bodies. Soon they were worn out from dress shopping and sat down in a café sipping a fruit cocktail watching life pass by. It felt like only a few seconds of peace and daydreaming had passed before they were interrupted by the manic pressing of a car horn and a voice shouting at them from a car door.

'Farooq, Fatima, Khadija, come quickly.' A young man from their village was shouting and waving at them from a taxi. 'All of you, your father has sent for you to come immediately. Something terrible has happened.'

Khadija instantly felt sick to her stomach. The lights. The hilltop. It was happening again.

They climbed in the car. 'What has happened?'

'Please tell us something,' Fatima pleaded. 'Anything.'

Faisal didn't say a word. His face was pale and his driving was erratic. The girls sat back down making *dua*, looking out of the window, straining to see ahead. It wasn't long before the plume of smoke streamed into the air, just as Khadija had seen it all those years ago.

Faisal dropped them near the scene. Farooq and Fatima ran off in an opposite direction, back towards their house. The neighbours were out on the streets, checking to see if all their children were accountable. They shouted for them over the fields, called out to them in their gardens, but as had happened too many times before, not everyone had returned. Khadija saw Saladin's mother. A young boy looked dishevelled. His forehead was cut. He ran straight to them. Khadija heard bits of what he was saying to them. She heard Karim, his brother's name, mentioned. Then she heard the name Saladin.

Now she was following the villagers as they went up through the streets, past her old home and past the cemetery. The last piece of land before the hills ascended up to the top of the turrets. Tyres were burning. The shadows were back on the hilltop. The nightmare was coming true once again, a nightmare she could never escape from. Khadija stopped dead. Her legs felt as weak as they did when she was a helpless child. But this time, there was nowhere to run. Lights and trucks were disappearing over the hilltop and there, as they dispersed, at the bottom of the hill was a body. A body of a boy.

Khadija hung back. Her feet physically unable to carry her any further. She heard them cry out and scream. But it was not Saladin's name they screamed. It was Karim. He was bleeding on the floor. 'Call an ambulance,' her mother shouted to the crowd of people behind, some already weeping, others leaving them behind and trekking down the fields and up to the hilltops, but they were dragged back down by others. Khadija covered her ears. She sat down on the cold hard ground as the light died in the distance. Karim was lying on the ground. He was now completely still. She knew how long an ambulance would take. His mother was left alone with him as the men went off. Others were following the tyre tracks in the dirt. His father was calling out for Saladin, who was nowhere to be seen.

Khadija went over and knelt by Umm Farooq. She was whispering over him and cradling his head in her arms. Khadija looked at Karim. Khadija took off her jacket and covered the hole in his stomach, but it soaked through. She looked at his face. Could she resuscitate him? Could she breathe her life into his lungs and save his mother and his family the trauma of losing their youngest boy? She pressed her fingers against his neck and tilted his head back, ready to breathe into him. She inhaled deeply and blew air into his lungs. His face rolled to the side.

'Enough, *habibte*. His soul has been taken. There is nothing anyone on earth can do now. He is with Allah.'

Khadija looked up to see if she could see an opening in the clouds.

'He's gone. They must have taken him.'

Khadija looked again. Had the darkness been the Angel of Death temporarily blocking out the sky? Was the land beneath them real? Could another soul have been taken from the hilltops? The few seconds where someone leaves this world behind and joins another passed between them. Amidst the smoke and mayhem, she searched for the trees to find a green bird, with another soul in its belly. She stared up to the clouds and saw a silhouette of a bird, soaring. Khadija brought her eyes down and saw Saladin's father. He looked at her briefly and then carried on talking in whispers to his wife. Khadija didn't want to believe it. Karim would wake up. Saladin would be on his way home, or in the village looking for them all. She stood up. Her clothes soaked, but because of the shock, she didn't notice. She began running back to the village.

'Saladin,' she shouted. 'Where are you?'

She ran into the courtyard of her family home. He wasn't there. She ran back towards the mosque. She ran into the men's prayer hall. He would be in there, making *dua* for his brother. He would be the responsible boy she knew, waiting so he could call the prayer and not be late for his job. Not to disappoint his father. He would be there. She wished it so hard. She ran to the mosque and up the stairs. But the room was empty.

She ran out onto the streets and shouted his name. She knelt on the lawn of her uncle's until his mother found her and took her into their home.

She gave her a new top to wear and poured hot tea with trembling fingers. The men came in and out. The ambulance had taken her son. She was waiting for the twins to come back. She wanted to be the one that they found out from. There had been no news of Saladin's disappearance. As Khadija sat there wondering, her mind raced. She imagined him in the mosque. She would walk in and find him in his place. Every time there was a knock at the door, she dreaded to think that another body of a boy was found, but there was no sign of him. As if he had vanished. She wondered if he had vanished, where he would have gone? Khadija thought of the bird in the tree. She would follow the bird and fly far away.

Chapter 19

KHADIJA STAYED IN THE family's house. Umm Farooq had told her to stay, an empty house was not good for her. Khadija accepted her invitation and passed through the days with them. She slept with their older sisters, Farooq and Fatima, in their room. She left early in the morning to walk past the mosque. She left before the dawn prayer in the hope that she would walk out onto the streets and hear Saladin's voice ringing faithfully from the minaret. Each morning she was disappointed. She carried on walking, her heart feeling heavier. Some mornings she would feel so overwhelmed at the size of the world and all its hiding places, that she would burst into tears, just doing normal, everyday things like standing in line at the bakery. Around her, people would utter gentle words of faith and strength.

This particular morning, she wandered through her old courtyard and to the broken remnants of the brick walls at the bottom and climbed higher until she could see out onto the fields. She wondered what she could expect to find but imagined that he may be there. She walked around the front of the house and back out into the street. She entered the cemetery and left her bread on the wall. She used both hands to hoist herself over where Saladin had shown her, landing in her childhood garden, this time during the daylight. The last abandoned garden in the neighbourhood was her own. Maybe Saladin was hiding, injured perhaps, behind the tall cypress trees there? Perhaps he was waiting for her to go there, to their old childhood places to tell her a secret he had discovered from the hilltops. Maybe his ghost was searching for her in a house that had been abandoned and left to time. The shade of the trees made it feel damp and cold. The earth below her feet was hard. She looked for someone living amongst the dead, but she was no closer to discovering his fate. The limbo she was in was almost harder to bear than a soulless body. At least that came with the relief of death, knowing you were in a better place. She would have preferred that Saladin was with his brother in paradise, soaring above the clouds in a painless eternity than trapped somewhere behind the hilltops.

Silently, she wandered around the place that had occupied so much of her dreams. The gardens were expansive just as she had been told and inside the brick walls were ancient apricot, fig and cherry trees amongst wild flora tangling over once man-icured courtyards and fountains. She spent time in the gardens, clearing away the regrowth and cutting back the weeds that had thrived. She uncovered gardening tools, that brought back to her young memories that were blurry but recognisable as her childhood ones. She found remnants of a family.

Around the courtyard, she stopped. Ahead of her, there were windows to an old house. It was a one-storey villa that wrapped around the gardens. It was the old house that was attached to where she used to live. It would have been beautiful in its day. Modelled on the older houses of Palestine, where the courtyard was a central feature and the rooms in the house all overlooked it. She walked around it. It had been abandoned for years. She walked inside the doors left open. Metal shells littered the floor. Dark stains crept around the house in its shadows. There was a young girl's room. A master suite with a silk bedspread still lying half on the bed but blackened from the years of dirt and exposure to the weather outside. This time, Khadija knew the house. There were remnants of its familiarity. She had an instinctive feeling this used to be home. She had broken down its walls and entered into her gardens. Saladin, despite his absence, had led her to them and she, at last, had discovered her ancestral home that had been hidden for most of her life. She had never felt ready to explore it fully before now, fearful of what might be found both in her past but also because of what future it might have meant for her. She was never ready before to take on a house that was robbed from them in the most tragic of ways. It was her against an army. After everything that had happened, what else could she lose? She didn't want to live her life afraid of shadows coming after her. Taking back what belonged to her was the first step in facing a fear that had followed her since the day of the fire in the *souk*. Khadija realised safety was never guaranteed. Even for the inconspicuous, because being born Palestinian meant you never could be.

***

Back at the house, they welcomed her despite the absence of bread. Khadija noticed that Umm Farooq could barely swallow. Khadija had felt that food was a luxury the dead couldn't partake in, so she too had felt too guilty to eat. She stayed in the kitchen and washed the pots, cut more salad and delivered it out to them.

'Come, Khadija, sit. Eat. You have been out all morning; you must be hungry.'

She watched as tears fell down Umm Farooq's cheeks but she didn't sob or wail. She just quietly grieved whilst feeding the family, clearing up and going about her daily duties. If the world started falling outside of the windows and the mountains began crashing down, the women of Palestine would still be cleaning the houses, preparing food, stitching dresses and rinsing blood from clothes.

The evenings were long. But so were the days. Khadija visited her childhood home, this time taking the keys and unlocking the gate instead of her favourite way in, over the walls with Saladin. She visited so often that she made plans on paper to restore it. She hired local builders from the surrounding villages to help her restore the house and gardens, ploughing her inheritance money back into her land. She hacked and hacked at the overgrowth, revealing more and more each day behind those concealed walls that eventually opened out into somewhere that became part of the present. It kept her brain active and it helped the days pass by quicker, so images of dead men didn't float in and block everything else out.

As she was clearing a particularly aggressive thicket from behind a cove, it gradually began to reveal something unnatural. Metal wire. At first, she couldn't work out what it was. The thorns scratched at her arms and the heat of the work left her exhausted, but she had to discover it. It rang in her distant memory and made her head hurt. *Revisiting places brings back your memory. Try and spend time in places that you have forgotten about.*

Behind the thicket, the metal wire began to take shape. An old aviary, empty of birds, only scattered with debris. Her eyes closed tightly under the shade of trees, her scar ached furiously. She had been there that night. She had fallen and cut her head as she ran away from the gunshot. It had ricocheted, she felt it in the wall in front of her. She felt the scar; she had fallen and cut her head on the corner of the wall. The incessant squawking of the bird's shrill panic deafened her. The blood disorientated her. She saw them in the distance. The shadows from the hilltop. Her mother's voice screaming out, 'RUN!' so she ran and ran through the alleyway that linked the houses. She pushed the huge gate shut to block out the sounds from the hilltop, the screaming birds.

She ran and ran past the graveyard, out onto the street. Unwittingly, she had followed her memory and was now standing back on the street alone. But today, it was decades later and there was no angel illuminating the streets.

She took a slow walk back to the house, praying that soon they would receive news of Saladin's whereabouts. She could tell him what she had seen. She could tell him of her plans.

She would only return to Saladin's home in the evenings, praying that there would be some news by the time she reached them. The night seemed to fall quickly. The streets were emptied. It was only the lights of the mosque, lighting up the green lights as a guide for travellers to find a place of prayer on their journeys. The *athan* was called out and the men walked to prayers. *If you walk through the darkness to the mosque, then your path to heaven will be paved with light.* After the worshippers had walked home, the doors were bolted. Dinners were taken inside. The courtyards were empty. The families were tense with the expectation that the skirmishes would bring the evil down into their homes and take away their youths in the middle of the night. It was something they had to be prepared for from when their children were born. It was a reminder that they didn't belong to them. They were their guardians for an appointed time and with that heavy responsibility, they would teach them as much as they could. They would guard their doors with their own bodies as the children lay in their beds, wondering if, in the distance, they could hear the sound of something coming to carry them away in the night. Khadija remembered her mother, Salma, in her wheelchair in front of the door. She heard her own mother's voice scream at her to run. Her last words to her child. Khadija had to distract her thoughts and each evening she sat with the women of the house and pulled out her wedding veil, her needle and the thick cotton thread and patch of waste canva to start her designs. Umm Farooq guided her and together they spoke about how she should be able to stitch her design across the bottom of the veil before the wedding. It kept their evenings used for distraction and work. The patience and focus on the stitching. One cross, combined with others forming the shape of wheat and cypress trees, replacing images of murder and prison cells the size of freshly dug graves.

After the agonising months of silence had passed, there was news that Saladin had been captured during the murder of his brother. He asked if they had captured Karim? Had they come to the house? She realised that Saladin, if he was alive, would have no idea that his brother wasn't. Saladin was alive. He was imprisoned a few hundred miles away from the village.

They become the men they are meant to be in prison. Do you agree with that, Khadija? They come out as soldiers. Look at our imprisoned, they become soldiers and scholars. Look at our streets, robbed and blood-stained. Look at our paradise. It is full.

The news of Saladin reminded her of the fragility of life. It reminded her of the promise she had made to Salma. The promise that she would take her to visit Al-Aqsa Mosque in Jerusalem. The realisation meant Khadija spent the last few nights in an uneasy state. She didn't want to go to Jerusalem. She didn't want to venture across the checkpoints and into the city where she knew she would not be welcome. There were so many soldiers there, maybe one would recognise her or her name. They would know she was the child that ran away and now they would take their chance to take her. But Khadija had learnt that to survive, she must face her fears at every single turn. She had tried running away, but they had only followed her.

Chapter 20

THE DAY ARRIVED AND Khadija boarded the bus to the city. It was a long drive and the heat as she descended, increased. The bus chugged along as if it too was struggling to make the journey. Khadija stared out of the window in anticipation of her day ahead. Her deep thoughts allowed the journey to pass easily and before she knew it, the bus pulled up the final hill before it stopped in Jerusalem. On the streets below her, the Dome of the Rock glistened. Khadija couldn't believe after all these years of seeing it on TV, that she was now here. A journey that had taken so long to come.

The passengers disembarked and walked the short trip to the first gate that broke through the huge towering cement wall that had been built through the city. A monstrous concrete snake, cutting up the land and severing the villages between it. Khadija stood looking at its imposing silhouette and then looked back towards the bus stop that would take her home. But even home wasn't safe, she thought. The stories she remembered came back into her head. The passages in the Quran. She had to do this so that she wouldn't spend her life running from her fears. She would no longer run away from what scared her.

She read messages of freedom that were sprayed onto the wall as she walked down a lane that tightened to an unnatural funnel neck. As she approached the first set of metal barriers, two soldiers stood in the booth, asking for her ID and the purpose of her visit. She handed them the travel pass to Al-Aqsa. She had been approved to go but that didn't always mean that you passed through unhindered.

Her heart quickened. She slowed it down with deep breaths. She looked around her at the solid objects to get some clarity. She was safe. She was passing through. She wasn't the child she was on the evening she escaped.

They handed it back to her and she passed through the first set. The checkpoint opened up to queues and gates and a larger cattle-style grid of barriers where each individual was stopped. Most were searched. Some were taken away. Some were refused entry. School children laughed and kicked each other in the queues, so used to this being their everyday. Khadija shuffled forward every time the queue went down. The heat was intensified by everyone crowding together. Men were searched. Women were stripped down to their underclothes behind screens. Children moaned. Babies cried, as they were hushed quiet and handed around to their siblings to amuse them whilst they waited. Over an hour passed. She fanned herself with her papers. She wondered why Salma had been so eager to make the trip.

The walls, the lights, the armed soldiers stood around the vicinity just like they did at home beyond the hilltops. Her turn at the main barriers approached. It was the final checkpoint for Palestinians entering the city. A few more turns and it was hers. The family in front of her passed through. The couple that came next were taken aside for questioning after they gave their name. It was her turn next. She was called forward. The guns from the soldiers hung by their sides, one hand was kept on them. She said her name. Her papers were checked. The cattle grid turned to allow her to pass. She walked forward. The green light continued to flash. She was through. A wave of relief rushed over her. They hadn't recognised her.

Everything faded into the background as she entered the ancient gates to the Old City, over a bridge that had been built centuries before to protect it. In that moment, she thought of Saladin; he was named after the saviour of Jerusalem. The famous warrior who reclaimed the city. As she meandered through, its stories came alive. The streets resembled what she was used to seeing on TV. They became the winding narrow streets stacked on either side with produce and traders selling their wares. She wasn't noticed in the bustle of crowds, tourists and traders shouting to be heard. Above their heads, old buildings with tiny windows concealed people's homes. Every inch of it was inhabited. She kept walking through the maze-like streets knowing they would all lead to its Holy centre. She could see it ahead of her. The streets narrowed, ahead it was just her and two soldiers guarding the door. This was her last fear. She walked with her head upright and stated her name clearly like it meant something, and it did.

They waved her through and the Noble Sanctuary opened up in front of her. There was no sound except for birdsong inside its haven. The paved pathway lined to her right with trees and to her left, stone buildings with dome-topped roofs. Ahead of her, the Dome of the Rock shone gold. Beautiful Arabic calligraphy adorned the Dome of the Rock's exterior. Inside, the stone was suspended in mid-air. The story of its ascension with the Prophet and there it was, plain for all to see. Its history, preserved. She passed by its central position in the courtyard and walked towards the steps leading down to Al-Aqsa Mosque. A fountain with running water for ablution was in front of it. She looked at the almost empty courtyard and remembered it during those Ramadan evenings packed full with worshippers, right up to its edges, the city of Jerusalem below it. She stopped for a moment to take it all in. She breathed in the air. It smelt different to home but there was a scent in the wind that had been carried as far as her home, she was sure of it. A sweetness that came only from lands that were as blessed as this. *This is the place where the sky will break open and the angels will come down.* She looked up to the sky, a lucid blue covered with dashes of clouds breaking her vision to the heavens. *There isn't a place in Al-Aqsa where an angel hasn't stood.* And the most famous story of them all, the night journey when Prophet Mohammed (peace be upon him) was taken by a winged creature from Saudi Arabia to Jerusalem and here to this spot. To Al-Aqsa Mosque and from there, he was taken with Angel Jibrael up to the highest heavens. Time and space seemed to halt itself there. A piece of land with so much history inside and outside of its walls. It was to be a place of salvation too, it was promised. And there she was, Khadija Hattam, standing upon its grounds. Khadija counted her footsteps into Al-Aqsa Mosque, savouring a long-awaited journey she was now blessed to make.

She slipped off her sandals and walked inside Al-Aqsa Mosque onto its red carpet. Elaborate lights lit up its interior as the hushed silence of the prayer filled the spaces. She completed her promise to her mother and never realised that by going herself she would link her past, her history and begin to have her fears alleviated in the same breath, because that was life. Land was passed on. Traditions and stories were passed on and no human on earth could prevent that. They could only strive to have something worth living for. She understood where people drew their strength in protecting this all because some things were worth more than they appeared. Khadija wasn't sure how long she sat there for, but she prayed for her parents, for Salma, for Saladin, for Palestine and for a future she was starting to see.

Chapter 21

BACK HOME, KHADIJA'S HOME and gardens were complete. On her instruction, the builders had removed the dilapidated house that Salma and Khadija had lived in. The courtyard was paved flat and led up to the front of her childhood house which could now be seen from the roadside. Its modest façade hid the wonder that lay out of the back of it, but it was no longer hidden. The metal sign of the family name was once again nailed to its exterior wall. *Bait Al-Hattam* had been restored to its rightful owner.

The wild flora from the garden was hacked back, allowing the sunlight to stream through the windows, lighting up the space and letting it breathe with fresh air. The house was mostly emptied of its contents. Not much had survived the elements. The windows, doors, floors and internal workings were fixed and restored. What was left behind were the bones of a home that Khadija had begun to make her own. The windows all around the house faced out onto the garden, and beyond the walls of the garden, the fields that were also hers. The outside space was where the house truly came into its own. The more it was lovingly restored, the more it captured Khadija's heart.

The gardens were manicured and an orchard of various trees bore fruits. Their roots must have been buried deep within the earth, drawing its own sustenance and keeping them alive and thriving through the seasons. Khadija was sure their smell had been what was carried through the wind to her as she explored the fields. She smiled, knowing that all this time they were closer than she imagined and yet she didn't know they existed. The courtyard was paved in old stone much like the stone she had seen in Jerusalem. The brick walls around the vicinity of the property looked like a newer addition, they hadn't aged as much on the field side, so Khadija assumed they had been built close to the attack. The walls on the left secured her border to the graveyards and the gardens and inside climbers had covered the cement in a web of green, now flowering white and purple flowers that fell over the walls.

Often, she wandered out into the fields and pulled the photograph out of her parents. She ran her hands over the grass, looking for something. Searching for a clue of what the ground might give away or of what the long meadow grass might be hiding underneath. But so many seasons had passed, time had washed away any trace of their ending.

In summer, the garden enchanted Khadija and she spent most of her time tending to it, hoping that when she saw Saladin again, she could show him what she had done. How it was unrecognisable to the one she stumbled into, but now it resembled what she was searching for all along. She came to realise that was why Amina had left her the Quran all those years ago. Her strength based on the faith and the power of Allah was always going to be enough. She had not seen it before despite her childhood spent in search of the signs of angels, or the green birds of paradise. She understood now that her home, her land, was her treasure. It was not under the walls like the orphans in the chapter of the Quran, The Cave, but it was within the walls; a treasure that had been preserved for her for the last decade, hidden. She knew she had nothing to fear now because she had never been alone. None of them were either in life or death. Despite the decades of neglect, of nature concealing it, of others trying to take it over. All the time that had passed and every event leading up to it and yet it was destined to be hers again.

As the summer days began to turn into autumn, the nights became shorter and the lights at the hilltop began to swirl over the top of the garden, but Khadija realised one evening when dusk fell, that the lights didn't fall into the garden. It was a slightly lower elevation and they skimmed over the top of it. The walls blocked out most of it and beyond them, the cypress trees that were planted decades ago had fulfilled their purpose and blocked out the view and the lights from the hill. She continued the work her parents had started. She had her own lights installed. Solar ones, powered by the strength of the sun.

The months passed and a cold, harsh winter blanketed the land with thick snow that Khadija had never seen the likes of before. It was so deep it came up to her knees. The snowdrifts built up outside the walls but Khadija felt safe inside, even alone, she felt as if the space was hers and of course she knew she wasn't alone. On nights when she couldn't sleep, she would wander out into the gardens realising that the rooftop was no longer there as it had been in her childhood. The building was gone. Just as the storyteller never seemed to speak as clearly as when she was a child, the voice hadn't returned as it used to then. Sometimes, Khadija would strain to listen in the dead of night when she couldn't sleep but all she heard were her own thoughts stirring in the night. Playing out in front of her, she saw the monsters from the hilltop, they merged with the ghosts of her and her ancestors' past, but she knew how to control it now. She knew there was a higher power and she was not a scared child anymore. The darkness was real but it was punctured with light.

Instead, Khadija would wander into her garden and sit watching the sky turn from black to navy to pink as another day rolled in. She searched in those dawn hours for the elusive green birds, but she never did see one again and wondered if it had all been part of her wild imagination.

Her *tatreez* now not only adorned her veil. It covered her entire dress. Ivory threads decorating the once plain gown, now shimmered in texture and light as it fell down the back of the gown and wrapped around its fabric. It told its own stories of her history and the women around her.

As winter was coming to an end, they received news that Saladin was going to be released. The days ticked by but Khadija never dared to let herself imagine seeing him again. She knew of the disappeared. They didn't always come home. She spent time with his family as they prepared the house. On the morning he arrived, she stayed away. She told herself it was to allow him to return in comfort but inside she was terrified that she would no longer recognise the man who had been imprisoned from the carefree boy she knew. She didn't know who he was anymore despite their continued engagement.

A few days had passed before she went to his home. He wasn't there so she passed her *salam* to the family and left a message for him to visit at his convenience. A few hours later, there was a knock at the door. Khadija's heart beat so loud she was sure they could hear it on the other side. She opened the door and was almost in a state of shock to see him standing there, in the flesh. She wanted to reach out and touch his face or hold both of his hands to feel their warmth. She reached her hand out but no one noticed amidst the excitement of his sisters, who stormed in, in a flurry of words about how amazing it was to have him home and how the wedding plans for the upcoming spring were back on. Wedding plans. Khadija felt as if it wasn't real. Nerves fluttered through her body in a chill. What if he felt different now? Did he still want to marry her? He caught her eye at that exact moment they said it and he smiled. It was the smile he saved for her. She had seen it throughout her life. In the school playground, in the streets as they played, on the steps of the mosque, when he delivered the letter. It was a smile Khadija had seen for many years so her heart began to rest. She hadn't lost him. She hadn't lost him to death and she had not lost him in life. His sisters pulled out magazines and pages they had saved and argued about the details whilst Khadija looked at her future husband. He looked different, older and thinner than when he had left but she would have recognised him anywhere. She felt guilty for thinking otherwise. All the negative thoughts she once had melted away in his presence.

As the moments passed by, Khadija didn't take another one of them for granted. Every time he spoke, she would watch him and savour his voice. Every time he laughed she wished she could capture it and keep it in a bottle in case it ever ceased. As with life, it had a tendency to resume despite the absences and precious moments that usually are missed in a heartbeat but not for Khadija. She relished every single one.

Saladin resumed his position in the mosque and when Khadija asked him about his time inside, he had said that he spent it making prayers for his brother. He didn't speak of it again. It was a part of his life. It was to be endured, as harshly as the wild winter storms and the days of release were likened to the spring and the birth of something new and hopeful. It was this hope and these moments of life that kept them alive.

***

And with the new and hopeful came the spring wedding. Khadija woke early. Her dreams were light and easily broken, morphing into the morning that was due to follow. So, Khadija shook off the blanket and woke up to pray the extra night prayer before it was time for dawn prayer. She hadn't been up at that time in a while but that time, in the last third of the night it was so peaceful and quiet. The birds hadn't started tweeting in the trees, the streets were empty as the worshippers hadn't begun to wake and wash for the first prayers at the mosque, so everything had a calm stillness. It was the perfect time for Khadija to lay her vulnerable heart open and leave it in Allah's hands.

As the morning opened up to the sounds of movement outside, Khadija made tea and sat at the kitchen table of her uncle's house. The house that was a part of her childhood. A chapter closing as she sat there on the morning of her wedding day and the last few hours she was to spend in the house. It dawned on her how momentous the occasion was for them to begin their life together. It was always going to be a day tinged with sadness because of the absence of the people she loved not being around to make it, but there was more happiness and hope than there was melancholy in her heart. And she had worked hard at trying not to let it seep in. She had been through so much, that deep down she knew Allah had always been there guiding her. And when she became lost, she had begun to find herself on a deeper level than she had considered before. She thought about Hiba at the Markaz Centre and the other sisters. She reminded herself about what Hiba had taught her on the condition of the heart and she had tried to make it softer. She had been mistaken to think it was its biology that took precedence when in fact, it was the heart and its condition, not only in its health but in its spiritual care that she had neglected for so long.

She wasn't sure if she was prepared for married life or if you ever could be. And after everything she had uncovered, after inheriting her home and the history of the parents, she knew that he was her future and he had been since she was a child.

A knock at the door interrupted her thoughts and brought the start of the morning to her. Amina rushed in, out of breath and slightly pink in the cheeks.

'I hope I'm not too late for a morning wedding!' she said, walking in, but almost instantly Amina's stride stopped dead. 'I suddenly remember visiting Salma here and working with her in her study. Do you mind if I go and take a look?'

Khadija left Amina to revisit the rooms of her friend's past and went to get ready in her bedroom. Amina came back to her there, tearful. But Khadija could tell like most of the women she knew, her tears had been wiped away to concentrate on the present. The past was gone.

'Wow, you look beautiful.' Khadija felt shy and didn't answer. 'How much did you pay for this work, it is stunning,'

Amina said, spinning her around and pulling out the fabric so she could see the stitchwork.

'I did it, Amina,' Khadija said quietly, but Amina had heard because Khadija noticed her eyes well up with tears once again. Her face said it all. Khadija allowed Amina to spend a few minutes turning the fabric and stroking the threads, appreciating her work, before Amina continued, 'Well I do recognise the place but it sure looks better with you here. Brighter. A woman's touch again just like when Salma was here.' Amina smiled and paused to look at Khadija on the cusp of becoming a wife. 'You know, Salma worked from her high school days in investigative journalism.'

'Yes, I am not surprised, looking at the work in her study.'

'She graduated top of her class. Much like you.'

'I am not sure I did actually, Amina.'

'Well, your class had one of the best results that year. Although, we are one of the highest educated in Arabia. We need to be, don't we? We have to build our own towns, take care of our own sick, teach our own children. I remember you always wanted to be a heart doctor. Do you think you will go back and complete your studies?'

'No, not to become a doctor. My heart yearned for something else. Biology couldn't fix it. It needed something from my soul which I have found now. My heart didn't feel the same when I left here. I missed every part of this place.'

'That is because you are part of your land, just like your parents were. And after all, without those that stay behind, we have no land. Look at Sidu Naser. He could move anywhere but he refuses to give up his home. Even empty houses are occupied. Why, even families living in homes built with their own hands are evicted. Here, the ordinary are the extraordinary because without us staying, there would be no Palestine left. The world may not see us, but Allah sees us.'

Khadija had never considered herself extraordinary but she understood now how the women in her life were. She remembered what her mother had told her as a child, 'When Allah loves you, even the angels know your name.'

'You will be moving out of this room, won't you?' Amina said, curling her hair in the mirror hung above the sink.

'Yes, I won't be living here, Amina.'

'Oh, yes, I suppose it makes sense to move in with Saladin, maybe to his parents' place, unless he has been building an apartment? Has he been building an apartment for you? I can't remember seeing any work going on at their place.'

'I am moving home, Amina. It is ready,' Khadija said, focusing on her reflection in the mirror.

Amina stopped curling her hair and squeezed her shoulders, 'And so are you.'

'You know I thought about those that fled Deir Yassin, those that turned up in villages like this one,' Khadija started.

'Just like your parents, your own mother couldn't finish her education because she cared for her mother after it happened.'

'I don't want to leave it all behind. I want to be there on those nights with my doors open. I don't want anyone to reach the end of our land and find no one there.'

'You have enough land. Maybe that is your future.'

Amina finished her hair whilst keeping an eye on the time and in the next moment, peered outside the windows to check the weather. But there was no need because the sun shone brightly, breaking through the young leaves and buds on the

221

trees, pouring into the room. Springtime rolled in from the tops of the heavens, caressing the earth with amber rays.

When Khadija was ready, they stepped outside and Amina went to take a photo of Khadija ready for the wedding.

'No, don't take one of me in front of my uncle's house. I want to look at it and remind me of where I am going, not my past.'

Khadija walked away from the house until she was in the street. She turned back to face Amina, with the rolling fields glinting in the light behind her. 'Here, this is the perfect spot.'

Amina's tears were already rolling down her face. 'May Allah bless you, you are so beautiful. Salma would have been so proud to see you today. The woman you have become. And I found this, Khadija, it is a newspaper article about what happened that night. You should have it.' Amina pulled out a newspaper article folded neatly from her pocket where she had reached for her tissues.

Khadija read the article and it told her what she had already seen. In black and white. Two Palestinian farmers, shot on their grounds. It was a story that had repeated itself for decades. She knew that her adopted mother Salma had kept her life hidden so she would be safe and she had done what she thought was right. Khadija understood now and was more grateful to her than ever that she should be found by such a mother.

'I was blessed to have two mothers.'

She walked down the streets, to the edge of the village. 'I thought it was in the fields opposite?' Amina asked.

'There was a change of location,' Khadija said, smiling.

Ahead she could hear the murmur of voices and the bustle of a crowd of people. She walked down and crossed over the patio of her childhood home. Khadija could see the gold and white wedding buntings strung between the cypress trees, fluttering gently in the breeze. The people she knew from the village rose from their chairs as she approached. She saw Sidu Naser had made it, her old teacher Miss Ayesha was there and Hakim. Her classmates, the future storytellers, pharmacists, doctors, teachers and engineers of the land. The entire village had made it.

At the front of her family's restored garden, a young man stood facing forward. His hands nervously went in and out of his pockets whilst his mother fiddled with his handkerchief that was posted in his suit breast pocket. His hair was neatly gelled back and Khadija smiled at the effort. She had never seen his hair styled like it before. The crowd, on noticing her presence, turned.

'She looks like her mother.'

'The gardens are just as I remembered.'

'*Alhamdulilah* they have been returned.'

She lowered her eyes and Amina lowered a white embroidered veil over her face. The crowd stood up and Saladin turned to look at her.

'Are you ready?' Amina said, linking her arm.

'My heart is,' Khadija said quietly. She glanced up to take one look at the moment so she could capture it for a lifetime. It was exactly like she had seen in her mother's wedding photographs. She looked up to capture the shade of the leaves, the angle of the sunlight, the feel of the air on her skin. She closed her eyes and breathed deeply, inhaling the scent of olives, apricots and figs. She glanced to the birds in the trees, in their new spring colours of pale yellows, browns and blues. But there amongst the branches, she saw something. She caught sight of a bird with bright green plumage. It stood still enough for her to see inside its wings. They were coloured black. It had a red blood-coloured breast and underneath it, its green neck and below its plumage, a long green tail. She stared for a moment, trying to catch her breath, tugging Amina's arm and pointing to the trees. 'The bird, Amina. I can see it. Its plumage is the colours of the Palestinian flag.'

'I know it well. It is the Quetzal bird. It is the bird of Palestinian freedom.'

'I recognise it. I have seen it before.'

'Of course you do, it is the one you tried to save from Taha all those years ago.'

'But I killed it.'

'No, the Quetzal bird kills itself in captivity. It is a fact known around the world. That's why it's illegal to keep them in cages.'

Khadija's eyes were brought out of the treetops by a sobbing coming from the guests. It was Aliya. 'I am sorry for everything, Khadija.'

Khadija didn't expect this, but she whispered back to her and squeezed her hand before continuing her slow walk down the long wedding aisle. Khadija had no enmity in her heart. Their childhood trivialities were now insignificant. They could leave their childish differences aside. They were no longer children of Palestine. They were the women of Palestine and they held its future between them.

She approached the end of the aisle, her wedding dress splayed out behind her adorned with the *tatreez* of her village, to an arch covered in leaves and fresh flowers. She looked upwards and saw the wings of the bird that she had searched for through her childhood. It was flying from tree to tree until it reached the expanses of rolling fields and disappeared into the clouds. Khadija remembered as a young child, asking the angels to take her far, far away like the birds. Not yet, she thought to herself, I have far too much to give first.

Saladin took her hand and her heart. Both were given freely. But her heart was not given entirely for Khadija had learnt that first and foremost, it belonged in part to its Owner.

A young woman called Khadija walked down the aisle in a town on the edges of the earth with one road in or out, cutting it off from the outside world. The hilltops rose and fell either side and sometimes the mist made it invisible to anyone below. If you search on most maps, you won't see the names of the towns or even know they exist. Steeped in tradition and age, they are kept alive by the people living within them. In a garden, in a restored house, there lives a family.

The night is quiet and still but if you listen hard enough you can hear the women of Palestine tell their stories.

We live in a land beneath the light. A heavenly light shaded from the harsh sun, basking in gardens of fruits and children. Our land, as tiny as a sesame seed, is our treasure.

The End

Afterword

The village and homes in my novel are based on family houses that I stayed in with my family in a rural village fifteen minutes outside of Ramallah in the West Bank. It is in the hills with an army base and settlement running around its circumference.

The village where my novel is set was kept nameless, because it could be any of the rural villages in Palestine; some no longer exist but remain so in memories and stories.

My Tata survived the Deir Yassin massacre as a young child.

The shooting of Karim is based on a shooting of a young boy who was shot dead at the border when we were staying in the house. It is such a regular occurrence throughout Palestine that it rarely makes the news.

The Quetzal bird is native to South America, but has been adopted as the National Bird of Palestine due to its plumage colours matching the Palestinian flag.

The importance of the land and traditions are key in keeping memories and Palestinian culture alive under a brutal occupation that discriminates Palestinians in every aspect of their lives and death. Narratives and history are an important source of information and under occupation, history is erased at an alarmingly high rate. This requires an urgency to capture it before it has completely been rewritten.

I wonder what Palestine my children will inherit as each time we visit, it has changed. I write down my family's stories and experiences so they can be shared as an authentic representation of our Palestine.

Mahmoud Darwish's poem, To Our Land, is quoted in the novel. For the poem in its entirety, visit poetryfoundation.org

Glossary

Allah: Arabic for God

Alhamdulilah: Praise be to Allah

Athan: Call to prayer

Dua: Supplicating to Allah

Fajr: Dawn, often used to refer to the obligatory prayer before sunrise

Habibte/habibe: Term of endearment female/male

In'shaa'Allah: Phrase meaning, 'If Allah wills'

Isha: Night prayer

Magrib: Dusk, often used to refer to the obligatory prayer at dusk

Muezzin: Person who proclaims the call to prayer

Riyal: Qatari currency

Salam: Peace (abbreviated greeting)

Salam alaikom: May peace be with you

Sheikal: Palestinian currency

Souk: Marketplace

Tata: Arabic word for grandmother

Tatreez: Traditional Palestinian embroidery

Wa alaikom salam: And may peace be with you

Other Books by
Shereen Malherbe

Jasmine Falling
The Tower
The Girl Who Slept Under the Moon
The Girl Who Stitched the Stars

Available from www.beaconbooks.net

Shereen Malherbe is a British Palestinian author. After spending over a decade living throughout the Middle East, Shereen now resides in England with her husband and four children.

Shereen has been a writer and researcher for various organisations including Muslimah Media Watch, Middle East Eye, Muslim Girl, Sisterhood Magazine and has also appeared on British Muslim TV and Islam Channel discussing the representation of Muslim women, resulting in her classification in the Media Diversified experts directory.

Shereen's debut novel, *Jasmine Falling*, has been voted among the Best Books by Muslim Women (Goodreads), and *The Tower* is now an academic set text in a US university. Her short story, *The Cypress Tree*, was recently published in World Literature Today's landmark edition, 'Palestine Voices'.

Lightning Source UK Ltd.
Milton Keynes UK
UKHW011815130922
408810UK00002B/309